Sweet & Tooth Spells

*Baking Up a Magical Midlife,
Book 4*

by Jessica Rosenberg

Blue
Octopus
Press

Published by Blue Octopus Press

www.BlueOctopusPress.com

(831) 471-7028

Library of Congress Control Number:

Library of Congress Cataloging-in-Publication
Data

Rosenberg, Jessica

Sweet & Sour Spells / Jessica Rosenberg

Copyright © 2023 by Jessica Rosenberg

Cover design by Karen Dimmick/Arcane Covers

I dedicate this book to the friends who have been by my side through the ups and the downs and who have believed in me every step of the way. I would not be where I am today without you.

Books feed your soul

the way food feeds your heart.

~ Jessica Rosenberg

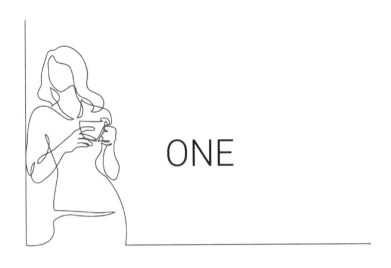

ONE

"Brrrr. It's cold out there." Hattie burst through the bakery door, letting in a gust of wintry air that made my skin prickle. She rubbed her hands together and stomped her feet on the mat. When I gestured to her head, brushed off the snow that had accumulated on her short spiky hair during her walk over.

Crystal glanced away from the fancy espresso machine that was the bane of my existence and smirked at the flowing tunic Hattie had paired with a pair of leggings. "No wonder you're cold. Who dresses like that in the middle of winter in New England? Where's your coat, woman?"

"My shop is four feet away! And I didn't realize it had started snowing. Again," Hattie grumbled as she waved hello to Amy. The latest addition to our friend group had arrived a few minutes earlier and had already claimed a seat at our usual table.

With a deft flick of her wrist that she swore had nothing to do with magic but none of us could replicate, Crystal added a final dot to the latte art on an oversize mug and pushed it across the counter. "This'll warm you up. Who else is coming today?" she asked, directing the question at me.

I placed the last of the pastries I'd prepared for the day in the display case and straightened up, wincing as my muscles protested how long I'd been hunched over. "Juliette just texted to say she was on her way, and Stacey, miracle of miracles, has taken the day off and should be here any minute."

"Did I hear someone say my name? Hope you're saying nice things about me." Stacey lost her fight with the wind and let the door slam shut behind her. She frowned at it as though it was solely responsible for the weather. "What the heck is this weather? Cassie, when you asked me to move up here, you never said anything about winter." She glared at me, but I knew it was in jest.

I grinned at her. "First of all, as grateful as I am that you've moved here, you know full well it was entirely your decision. Second of all, everyone knows about winter. It's a pretty big deal around the world."

"We didn't have winter down in Georgia," she grumbled, hanging her coat up on the antique wooden coat rack that had appeared the instant the weather had turned cold. There were days when living in a semi-sentient building had its perks. Oh, who was I kidding? Having a home and shop that anticipated our needs was never not incredible.

"We had winter in Georgia. But you had a knack for jetting off to warmer climes whenever the thermostat dipped below 45." My tone might have been snarky, but there was no bite to my words.

Stacey brightened and grinned at me. "Oh yeah! Good thing my editor is sending me to Bali on Monday. I can't think of a better time to go lounge in the sun."

As a travel photographer, Stacey got to visit the coolest places and call it work. She'd only recently moved up to Boston to take a new job as a staff photographer for a start-up digital travel magazine and had been face-down in work at the home office since she'd arrived to help them get up and running.

"You're going to Bali? Take me with you?" Hattie asked, looking into the distance with a beatific expression on her face like she was already on a warm, sunny beach soaking up some rays.

"How are you at carrying heavy photo equipment?" Stacey replied, only half joking.

Hattie's expression fell and the corner of her mouth quirked up in a self-deprecating sneer. "Not good. My back would probably give out after three feet. It's a good thing I have young people to help me in the shop or things would be dire." She winked at me, and I laughed. One of her 'young people' was my twelve-year-old daughter.

Which reminded me...I walked over to the swinging doors to the bakery kitchen and yelled up the stairs to our apartment, "Aurie! Are you up? You're going to be late if you don't get a move on!"

The sound of grumbling and puppy feet pounding across the floor reassured me that she'd at least gotten out of bed. That was the biggest hurdle. I'd go up in a bit to see if she'd eaten enough to keep her functioning until lunch and to make sure she had dressed appropriately for the snow that seemed intent on coming down despite what the weather forecast had promised. Much like Stacey, Aurie wasn't taking to winter well and had already lost three hats and four pairs of gloves.

Pushing away a prickle of irritation over her carelessness, I stepped back into the bakery and let myself forget everything about moody teens, missing winter wear, and disruptive puppies. We only had about a half hour until the bakery was officially open and I wasn't about to waste a minute of it.

For months, my friends and I had been gathering for coffee and laughs before our respective stores opened. Our group was informally referred to as 'the Brewhahas,' an apt name that never failed to bring a smile to my face.

"I have exciting news!" Amy was saying when I sat and wrapped my hands around the large mug Crystal had placed in front of my usual seat. While I waited for her to elaborate, I lifted my drink to my nose and took a deep sniff. Mmm. Peppermint. Crystal had hit it out of the park with this one. It would be all over our fans' social media feeds by the end of the week. Ideas for complementary cookies started flashing through my mind. "I signed a lease this morning!"

Without being too obvious about it, I snuck a glance at Crystal while everyone else cheered. They'd been pussy-footing around each other since we'd first met Amy at the Portney Brews & Hues fall festival. Much to everyone's delight, Amy had come back to visit between art festivals and holiday craft fairs, both to hang out with us and to explore her nascent magical abilities. Their attraction had deepened with each visit, but to the best of my knowledge, they still hadn't acted on it. If she was making Portney her official home base, maybe that was no longer true.

The blush that turned her ears pink when I caught her eye made me snicker and clap my hands together with glee. "Did it finally happen?" My eyes danced from Crystal's mortified face to Amy's baffled one.

"How did..." Amy started asking. She stopped when she saw the look on Crystal's face and chuckled. "Yes, we finally went out, and I'm staying in town. Draw your own conclusions." She winked at Crystal and reached over to squeeze her hand. When Crystal replied with a broad grin of her own and let their hands stay clasped together, my heart soared.

Amy had proven to be an absolute delight. She was funny and sweet and easy to get along with. More importantly, Crystal lit up like the Rockefeller Center Christmas tree whenever she walked into the room.

"What'd I miss?" Juliette's voice cut through the cacophony of excited chatter a moment before the slam of the door caught everyone's attention.

With her usual bluntness, Hattie recapped the conversation. "Amy and Crystal finally did the deed, and Amy signed a deed. Ok, a lease, but that wasn't half as fun to say."

Juliette's eyes widened and her mouth dropped open. "Wow! That's fantastic! On both counts!" If I hadn't been looking right at her, I would have missed the flicker of longing that flashed across her face, but by the time I narrowed my eyes to glean more information, she looked as happy as everyone else in the room.

After stomping the snow off her feet and hanging up her coat, she joined us at the table. In a near-perfect imitation of my earlier move, she picked up her mug and gave it an appreciative sniff. "Oh! Peppermint!"

Crystal beamed. "It's a new blend. I used some of the fresh mint Cassie's produce guy brought by last week. Let me know what you think."

"Well, so far, I think it smells delicious," Juliette replied with a grin. "I hope it's strong. I'm going straight to an estate sale from here, and I'm a little worried about driving through the snow."

"Is this one for fun or for a client?" I asked. After accidentally coming across some old family papers at her first estate sale, she was starting to make a name for herself in the witching circles as a finder of missing grimoires and magical artifacts.

"Both." She grinned. "You know how I feel about digging through old books and letters."

I suppressed a shiver. "Better you than me!"

For a few moments, the conversation flowed around me, and I let myself bask in the happy sounds of friendship. All my favorite people were here with me, enjoying each other and their breakfast. The homey scent of cinnamon, peppermint, sugar, and vanilla from the drinks and pastries I'd baked earlier surrounded us, and the happy sounds of chatter and laughter warmth wrapped themselves around me. It had taken me so long to find the place I truly belonged, and it was exactly as sweet as I'd always imagined it would be.

"Did you all hear what happened to Margie's greenhouse?" Hattie's voice rose above the hubbub drawing everyone's attention.

"I heard someone mention something about it yesterday, but I got sidetracked before I could get any details." Crystal said cocking her head to the side. "What happened?"

"Well," Hattie said, leaning back in her seat and crossing her ankle over her knee. A mischievous twinkle in her eye gave her the appearance of a cat relishing his catch. "I was over at the garden center picking up some straw for the rabbit hutches and overheard someone say that everything in her greenhouse died overnight. One moment her plants were lush and healthy and the next, poof! Everything was rotten."

"Did her heater fail or something?" As the only non-witch at the table, it would never have occurred to Stacey that a technological mishap couldn't have decimated Margie's magically nurtured plantings.

"Nope!" Hattie's face shone with suppressed delight. "One day the plants were fine, the next day everything was dead. It seems even her seeds are rotten! Can anyone spell 'Rule of Thirds?'" She quirked an eyebrow in the air and gave us all a pointed look.

"You really think that's it?" Crystal asked, her forehead creased in a frown. "Don't you think it would have happened sooner if that were the case?"

It had been months since Margie had poisoned Aurie. While I was busy in the bakery, she'd snuck into the kitchen and left a pretty little bottle containing a potion designed to make me a little ill. Her intention had been to 'teach me a lesson about defying her,' but Aurie and her friends had found the bottle before I even saw it. On a dare, Aurie had drunk the whole thing and ended up in a coma.

"What's the Rule of Thirds?" Amy asked, her face creased in a small frown. "Wait, you mentioned something about that when you first explained magic to me," she said to Crystal, "but I can't remember the details."

"Simply put," Hattie said in her best 'time for a magic lesson' voice, "intentions matter when it comes to magic because everything comes back to you threefold. Positive magic boomerangs back as positive energy. Ill-intentioned magic..." her voice trailed away, and she raised her eyebrows suggestively. "You get the picture."

Amy's eyes widened.

"Well, here's hoping this keeps her busy and her attention away from me for at least a few days." I raised my mug in a toast. "I could really use some time out from under her constant disapproving glare."

TWO

"What does a man have to do to get a cup of joe 'round here?" My father grumped, pushing through the swinging doors from the bakery kitchen.

"Good morning to you too, Hugh," Crystal replied with a laugh before pointing to the fresh pot of coffee sitting on the warmer next to the espresso machine. This exchange had occurred every morning since my father had moved in following a bad fall caused by out-of-control blood sugar levels. The trucking company he'd worked for most of his life had let him go, claiming he was a liability because he was having trouble managing his diabetes while on the road. The lure of a portion of Great Aunt Bea's estate had brought him to my doorstep, and I had convinced him to stay with us while he recovered from his accident.

Instead of his usual snippy comeback, he grunted at Crystal in reply, and I watched him make his way behind the counter.

Acting like an old grump was part of his schtick, but over the last few weeks, we'd all gotten to know him better and could see right through the facade. He had a coffee machine in his apartment, he came down for the banter. So where was the back and forth this morning?

I knew he hated it when I hovered, but I couldn't help worrying about him. A solitary life on the roads had taught him abysmal self-care habits, and I was terrified his diabetes would get out of hand if I didn't watch him like a hawk. It wasn't a great way to nurture our burgeoning father/daughter relationship, but I didn't have the words to express the pit that formed in my stomach at the thought of losing him after having spent so many years without him. So, I hovered, he grumbled, and we both pretended that was how things were supposed to be.

"Good morning, Dad. How'd you sleep?" I called without expecting much of a response, but when he didn't even deliver his usual grumble about minding my own business, I frowned. "Dad? You okay?"

He finished pouring coffee into a mug and, without turning around, waved just two packets of sugar over his head so I'd see he was being reasonable. The fact that he wasn't making a fuss over how sweet he was making his coffee only increased my worry. It wasn't like him to not negotiate a third packet.

I was still debating whether getting up to go talk to him would make things worse when he picked up his mug and turned around. He'd filled it to the brim, so he took a sip, grimaced at the taste, and rolled his eyes at me when he caught my worried frown.

"Stop fretting, buttercup," he said, walking around to the front of the counter and leaning back against it. He'd been testing out nicknames for me and had yet to find one we both liked. The chuckle he let out at my grossed-out face eased a lot of my concern. "Before you ask again, I slept fine, my blood sugar is text-book perfect, and I am doing nothing at all exciting that could possibly affect my health. He hid his expression behind his mug, but I saw the way frustration tightened his eyes as he finished his sentence.

"Nothing at all, eh?" I teased as my brain spun, trying once again to come up with something for him to do. He hated working in the bakery, though, to be fair, bussing tables and sweeping up after customers was hardly scintillating work. There didn't seem to be much available for a man whose work experience was limited to driving a big rig, though.

His usual expressionless mask gave way to a soft look that didn't appear often. "Stop worrying so much, kid. I'm fine. A little bored," he half shrugged, "but fine. What're you all nattering on about over there?" He gestured with his chin to our table where the rest of the Brewhahas were still discussing whether they'd seen evidence of the Rule of Thirds working against Margie over the last few months. Before I could answer, Aurie barreled through the swinging doors, one arm stuck through her favorite sweatshirt and Willow, her not-so-little-anymore golden-haired mutt puppy at her heels. Given that the pup's mother had been a rescue and the father a mystery, it was still unclear how she would end up looking, but I had a hunch she'd eventually turn out to be a small pretty, off-brand Golden Retriever. She certainly had the loving goofy personality of a real one.

Aurie didn't even give me time to tell her she needed to wear something warmer and to get the dog out of the bakery.

"Mom!" she whined, stomping her foot like she was closer to nine than thirteen. "They're going to cancel the field trip!"

My mind raced through the endless list of things I had to remember before hitting on what I thought she might be talking about. "Tuesday's field trip to Walden Pond?" I glanced at the still-falling snow and scrunched up my nose. I couldn't fault the teacher; the last place I wanted to traipse through was a soggy, icy forest next to a large frozen lake. Just the thought made me shiver.

"The email headline said there was no bus driver!" Her indignation was still coming out as a high-pitched whine, so it took a moment for her words to register.

"Email headline?" I narrowed my eyes at her. "What were you doing on my computer?"

"Mom…" How the kid could make a single-syllable word sound like it had five was baffling to me. "That's not the point! We were going to look for owl pellets! And look for hibernation dens!"

I set my irritation aside and focused on what she was saying. She'd been harping on about the field trip for weeks, and I could see tears forming in the corners of her eyes. "I'm sorry, bug. That really sucks."

"Hey! We agreed! If I can't say 'sucks,' you can't either!" she protested as I stood and started to usher her back toward the swinging doors. Crystal saw me heading that way and winked. It was nice to know she had my back if it took me a little longer to get Aurie going than usual.

I glanced at my dad on the way past and almost stopped to ask about the calculating look on his face, but getting Aurie ready for school trumped whatever was going on there.

"You're right. I'm sorry. That's a real bummer. But tell me, have you had breakfast yet?"

Aurie had her snow boots on, and we were halfway through a heated discussion about whether or not a sweatshirt was a sweater when a bloodcurdling shriek from the commercial kitchen derailed my train of thought. My assistant-slash-bread-baker, Christina, wasn't the screaming type, so I was on my feet and running before the tail end of her shout died out.

Taking the stairs three at a time wasn't the greatest idea for someone who had a tendency to twist her ankles, but it wasn't pain that stopped me dead in my tracks at the bottom. I had once traipsed along the Mexican coast for hours to witness a geological marvel that made water shoot up twenty feet in the air every time a large wave hit the cliff 'just-so.' This was more impressive. Where my gorgeous, brushed steel industrial faucet should have been, a geyser of water was shooting straight up to the ceiling. The faucet, I discovered after looking around wildly, had landed clear across the kitchen. The counter around the sink was already inches deep in water and the rest of the kitchen was well on its way to following suit.

Christina had stopped shrieking and progressed to moving the bread racks out of the spray, but from the looks of it, salvaging all her hard work was a lost cause.

"Oh, no!" Darting past her, I ran to the sink and smashed my hands over the spout. Maybe if I pressed down hard enough, I could contain the water long enough for someone to shut off the water mains. It was like trying to stop a train with my bare hands. Water seeped through my fingers and fought my hands as I tried to find a way to position them so my fingers wouldn't get ripped off.

"Can't you... you know, pause things?" I called over my shoulder to Christina when it became obvious there was no way my hands were going to stem the powerful spout. "I can go turn off the water mains, but your magic would buy me some time."

She shot me an exasperated look. "You think I didn't try that?" When she saw me frown over my shoulder, she heaved an annoyed sigh. "I know we agreed I'd never use my magic here, but extenuating circumstances and all that. Anyway, it didn't work. I have no idea why."

"What's wrong?" Crystal burst through the doors with the rest of the Brewhaha crew and my father hot on her heels, just as I grabbed a dishcloth. I wadded it up and tried to stick it in the hole the water was gushing out of, but all I managed to do was make the water spray toward me instead of straight up. Sputtering, I let go, and the water shot up again.

"It's like the water pressure got crazy high all of a sudden. Grab as many dishcloths as you can and try to keep the water from going into the bakery." The floor all around me was soaked and the water level was starting to rise. "Dad? How're your plumbing skills? Think you can find the water mains and shut it all down?"

A panicked expression crossed his face, but he nodded. Rolling her eyes, Hattie hurried off after him. I could only hope that between the two of them, they'd figure it out. In the meantime...

"Juliette! Can you use your water magic to, I dunno, slow things down?"

Her eyes widened and she pulled her mouth back in a grimace that didn't instill confidence, but she clenched her teeth and braced herself. Of all my friends, Juliette had the weakest elemental magic, but she was the only one of us with any water magic at her disposal.

For a moment, it seemed like the stream of water was wavering, and I held my breath. Then, Juliette let out a little gasp and the water shot up just as straight and strong as before.

"I'm sorry. I don't know what's wrong. My magic is never super powerful, but it's like I can barely access it."

I glanced away from the water long enough to see how red her face had gotten and noticed the sheen of sweat on her brow.

"That's weird. Christina couldn't access hers at all." I didn't have time to test my own air powers before the rushing water suddenly stopped. The silence that filled the kitchen was deafening. For a moment, all we could hear was the steady flow of water cascading over the edge of the center console hitting the ocean that covered my kitchen floor. The floor was covered in at least two inches of water. Every surface was wet and the loaves resting on the cooling racks were soaked beyond redemption.

The only good news was that Crystal had managed to stuff enough dishcloths under the door to keep the water in the kitchen, and I'd hauled the day's pastries into the bakery long before the water show began.

"Well, crud." I pushed my sopping wet hair out of my eyes and sagged against the counter.

Juliette, Crystal, and I were still standing, our mouths hanging open when Hattie and my father rushed back into the room.

"Did we stop it?" Hattie asked, gasping for breath. "That damn water main is all the way on the other side of the yard." She stopped talking and looked around. "Well... crud."

"My words exactly," I said.

"That is going to be a bear to clean up," my father added, not all that helpfully.

"Good thing you had nothing going on today, right?" The look on his face made it clear he didn't find me nearly as amusing as I did.

THREE

"**D**o you think the pipes froze? Because an explosion of that caliber would create a catastrophe of unfathomable proportions in my bookstore." Juliette's eyes widened and the corners of her lips turned down. She glanced in the direction of her store as if she could see any potential damage through the buildings.

"The pipes looked fine to me," Hattie said, but the anxious look on her face when she glanced over at her own shop, belied her statement. "But I think I'll feel better if I double check." Without another word, she bustled out of the kitchen and hurried through the bakery. We all looked at each other as the bells over the door jangled.

When it jangled a second time, Crystal frowned. "It's a little early for a customer, isn't it?" She glanced at the clock and pushed the swinging door open. "Great. That's just what we needed," she muttered under her breath. An annoyed 'harumph' clued us all into who was dropping by unannounced.

Juliette's face fell. "I'll go. I'm sure she's here for me."

Margie probably was hunting down her granddaughter, but seeing as she was standing in my shop, it would have seemed rude for me to let Juliette greet her on her own. Margie hated me enough as it was, I didn't need to give her another reason to be annoyed at me.

As the owner of the building that housed Juliette's bookstore, and because of the minimal rent she required from her, Margie took tormenting Juliette as her due. She was prone to acting as though she was owed not only respect but also Juliette's undivided attention whenever she desired.

Juliette's shoulders inched up as she stepped through the door and greeted her grandmother, but I knew she wasn't letting any anxiety show on her face. Margie could smell fear and trepidation a mile away and was skilled at exploiting it.

"Good morning, Grandmother."

Margie's answering glare wasn't directed at me, but a chill still ran down my back.

"I need you to clean out my greenhouse today." The town matriarch's face was mostly covered up by a ghastly hand-knit scarf wrapped around it, but there was no missing the smoldering rage in her eyes and the way her nostrils were flaring. She was often angry, but this seemed a little worse than usual. "I expect it to be done by the end of the day."

Out of the corner of my eye, I saw Juliette blink at her a few times, as if expecting an explanation, but she should have known better. A dozen retorts flew through my head, not one of which would serve Juliette in any way. As she took one measured breath after another without taking her eyes off her grandmother, the tension in the room ratcheted up. Margie's gaze narrowed and there was no doubt they'd both forgotten I was standing right next to them.

I wanted to think that in Juliette's shoes, I would tell Margie exactly what she could do with her demand, but even though I didn't rely on her for my livelihood, the old witch still terrified me. Until she'd poisoned Aurie, I'd had a healthy respect for her magic. Since then, I'd grown a lot more leery of her abilities. She'd shared that she had only dabbled in black magic once, when she'd been a young witch, but part of me had wondered if it was really true.

Glancing out the window toward her bookshop, Juliette's shoulders slumped as the fight seeped out of her. One day she'd have the courage to stand up to her overbearing grandmother, just not today.

She opened and shut her mouth a few times before looking at the ground and replying in a meek voice. "I'm sorry, Grandmother, I have plans already today."

"Such as?" She arched an eyebrow like she couldn't wait to hear what Juliette thought was more important than doing her bidding.

"Well, for one, I have some errands to run this morning." It didn't surprise me that Juliette wasn't mentioning the estate sale. She hadn't told her grandmother she was expanding her business to keep her from interfering or finding a way to mess things up for her.

The arch in Margie's eyebrow morphed from amused to intrigued, and I focused on the way the counter was digging into my hip so I wouldn't give in to the urge to throw myself in the line of fire to protect my cousin for the scathing reply I was sure was coming. Juliette pulled a little of the boldness out of her tone. "And of course, I have the store to run."

"Oh, your little shop, pfft." Margie waved her hand dismissively. "I can't fathom anyone will care or even notice if you close for a day or two."

Simmer down, Juliette. Don't give her any unnecessary ammo. The more she thinks you care about the store, the more she'll use it against you, and you know it. Without telepathic powers, there was no way Juliette could hear my thoughts, but I beamed them in her direction anyway.

Whether she heard me or instinctively knew she'd gone too far, Juliette gave Margie her blandest smile and started fumbling in her coat pocket for her keys. "Oh, I'm sure a few people would be put out if I closed my shop for a day or two." I had a feeling the snow might put a wrench in her store's regular schedule, but I didn't let my doubts show on my face. There was always a chance people would show up.

Sidestepping her grandmother, Juliette continued, "I have a toddler reading group later this morning and the Space Opera book club meeting in the late afternoon." She cocked her head as if mentally reviewing her to do list. "Oh, and I have to ship out a few online orders. If I don't get them out today, I might not have enough to pay my rent on time this month."

I bit back a smirk. That last bit was a blatant lie. Juliette had inherited a little nest egg from our great-aunt. I wasn't all that surprised that she'd kept the information from her grandmother. There was no telling what Margie would have done if she'd known about the money.

Margie made another dismissive sound. "Cancel all that nonsense. I need you there in ten minutes."

When Juliette glanced in my direction, I saw a flash of defiance I hadn't expected. "I'm sorry, Grandmother. I can't do that. People are counting on me. I promised a regular client that I'd go with her to an estate sale this morning to evaluate a book she'd like to purchase. If you still need my assistance come Sunday, I'll be more than happy to help you then."

Margie's eyebrows shot up in surprise and she reared back, her eyes wide with feigned hurt. "Just to be clear, you are refusing to help me, your own flesh and blood, who is getting up in age and can no longer do much with her increasingly frail body, in her time of need, so you can respond to the request of a complete stranger?" Her lower lip quivered, and it took near-superhuman effort to not roll my eyes at her helpless old lady act. There wasn't a weak bone in her entire body.

Juliette's smile looked a little forced. "It's not like that at all. Of course, your needs matter to me. But I made a commitment to these people, and it would be terrible for my reputation if word got around that I was no longer reliable."

Margie stuck her nose in the air and sniffed. "Well, I see how it is." She turned and walked a few steps before spinning back around, her usual calculating look back in her eye, no trace of the hurt grandmother remaining on her face. "One day I'll be gone, and you'll be sorry. Just you wait and see." With a satisfied 'harumph' she turned back around and stormed out of the shop.

Juliette watched her negotiate the icy sidewalk and waited until she was out of sight before heaving a sigh of relief and shooting me a sheepish smile. "I definitely will NOT be sorry the day she's gone."

I snorted. "You and me both."

FOUR

Not only was the only plumber available on such short notice exorbitantly expensive, but he found nothing wrong with the pipes. He replaced the faucet and turned the water back on, looking at me askance the whole time. If there hadn't been half a dozen witnesses, I'd have thought I was losing the plot by the time he left me standing in ankle-deep water.

If my magic had been working properly, cleaning up the damage would have been a snap, but I couldn't get the air to cooperate long enough to sweep the water out the kitchen's back door. Every time I tried, the air doubled back and flicked water in my face. With the bakery already an hour behind schedule, the bread a soggy mess, and the last of my nerves about to snap, I almost walked away, but I didn't want to tempt fate. With my luck, mold would start growing before I said goodbye to the last customer of the day. I grabbed my phone and shot Hattie a quick text.

Help! How do I clean up this disaster?

If anyone knew, it would be her. Surely, she'd had to clean up more than the occasional spill in her pet shop. I was still staring at my phone, waiting for a reply, when Hattie poked her head through the back door.

"With this." Without stepping into the water, she held out a broom with a rubber squeegee head.

"Ah! Yes! That's perfect. Thank you!"

She stayed long enough to make sure I had a handle on the situation, then left me to the task at hand. It didn't take me long to regret sending Christina home for the day. She'd been drenched, upset, and frustrated, and even though our customers wouldn't be thrilled about the lack of bread, it wasn't like she'd be able to recreate hours of work in minutes. Sending her home until it was time to work on afternoon prep had seemed like the least I could do.

By the time I got most of the water cleared up and disposed of the ruined bread, chatter had started trickling through the swinging doors. I reluctantly turned my back on the rest of the clean-up to go help Crystal deal with the customers.

"Is everything okay back there?" A woman standing at the counter craned her neck so far to peer through the swinging doors, I was worried I'd have to call her a chiropractor. She was a regular and one of the biggest busybodies in town. Once she left, word of our watery disaster would reach every far corner of town within minutes.

"Nothing a little mopping up can't fix." I smiled and handed over her usual order. "Actually, Lori, could you do me a huge favor? Do you think you could spread the word that we have no bread today, but we'll be back to our regular menu tomorrow?"

She gaped at me for a moment, teetering between being offended at the insinuation that she was adept at spreading gossip and being willing to accept the truth for what it was. I held her gaze until she landed on acceptance. With a shrug and a self-deprecating chuckle, she nodded. "Sure thing, love. Anything for the best baker in town."

Her phone was in her hand before she'd gotten a foot away from the counter.

"Well, that's one thing taken care of," Crystal said. She looked as exhausted as I felt, but since she hadn't spent the better part of a half-hour sweeping water out the door, I decided teasing her was fair game.

"So? Late night yesterday? Eh?" I poked my elbow into her side and raised an eyebrow suggestively. Watching the blush roll across her face was more satisfying than it should have been.

"Know what the drink of the day is called?" she replied, dancing out of the way of my elbow.

"No, what?" I asked with a frown.

"A big ol' nunya business latte with extra foam. Would you like one?" She shot me her most saccharine smile and batted big, innocent eyes at me.

"Touché." I laughed and turned my attention to the next customer in line. If she wanted to keep her date details to herself, that was her prerogative. "But in case you've forgotten, I'm going on a date with a certain delicious lawman tomorrow. If you want details, you better be willing to pony up, if you know what I mean."

"Oh, I'm delicious, am I? Or are you going on a date with someone else tomorrow?" Sam asked, walking up to the counter, his eyes dancing with delight.

Crystal's burst of laughter turned all the heads in the bakery. Which was nice, because it meant everyone in the room witnessed my face catch on fire. Luckily for me, and everyone around me, my face didn't actually burst into flames. Less luckily, the ground didn't open up beneath me to spare me the embarrassment of meeting Sam's amused gaze.

"I... ah..." I opened and shut my mouth and tried to think of anything I could possibly say to walk back what I'd said, but I drew a complete blank. Even the song that had been looping around in my head for the better part of a week was gone.

Sam leaned closer and whispered low enough that not even Crystal heard, "for what it's worth, I think you're delicious too." A hint of sweetness dancing on my tongue made me realize my mortification had made my mental shields drop, and I could taste how amused he was by the whole situation. His delight tasted like cotton candy and for a second, I wondered if it was how his mouth would taste if, *when*, we finally kissed.

"Ahem." Miss Bitsy's discrete throat clearing snapped me to my senses, and we jerked away from each other.

The usual bakery hubbub came back into focus and for a second, everything seemed louder and brighter than it should have been. My heart hammered in my chest as I struggled to get my breathing under control. At least Sam's face was the same color mine felt, and he looked just as discombobulated by how close we'd been to letting our lips touch.

He recovered faster and tipped his hat at me with a grin and a wink. "Let's try that again tomorrow, shall we?" He grabbed the to-go cup Crystal handed him and sauntered out into the cold. I knew I wasn't imagining the cocky hitch in his step.

While a thousand butterflies woke up and started rioting in my belly, parts of my body I'd long thought dormant started to tingle as I watched him walk away.

"Did that just happen?" I hissed at Crystal while getting Miss Bitsy her regular morning treat.

"Do you mean, did you almost just kiss everyone's favorite deputy sheriff right here in the middle of the bakery while half the town looked on? Because if so, then yes, yes it indeed just happened," she replied, her eyes dancing with delight.

"Can this day get any worse?" I groaned. When she laughed in response, I pushed all thoughts of sexy lawmen and water damage out of my head and turned to the next customer in line. Serving people good food was one thing I knew I couldn't get wrong.

FIVE

According to Murphy's law, the day should have gotten significantly worse after my flippant comment, but much to my chagrin—because I had nothing to distract me from an endless replay of the near-kiss—for once, everything went according to plan. Customers weren't overly upset about the lack of bread. Aurie came home from school and didn't put up a fight about tidying her room. She even ate the meatloaf I prepared for dinner without so much as a single complaint.

Even Stacey had been taken aback. "Think she's coming down with something?" she asked as Aurie and Willow scampered off to watch a TV show on my laptop before bed. Most evenings, if she'd finished her homework and her room was somewhat tidy, we watched something together on the family room couch. However, since Stacey was spending the weekend, and we were camped out on the couch, it only seemed fair to allow her the rare indulgence of getting to watch something in her room.

"I don't think so," I frowned looking down the hall as though I could see through Aurie's closed door.

"If it's not that, then maybe it's that she can tell her mama is out of sorts tonight?" Stacey's voice rose at the end of her sentence and she glanced at me out of the corner of her eye.

"I am not!"

"Okay, fine, how about... distracted? Can we say that?" she asked, pouring herself another glass of wine and scootching back into the corner of the couch. "Wanna tell me all about it?"

"I don't know what you're talking about," I protested.

"Sure. And a certain good-looking man in a uniform didn't almost ravish you on your bakery counter earlier today?"

"He did not!" My cheeks heated up and I tossed a cushion at her.

"Whoa! Careful with the wine! Wouldn't want to waste any!" Stacey batted the cushion out of the way before it could connect with the glass. "So, what did happen?"

"Obviously, you know what happened." I rolled my eyes and sighed. "Did Crystal tell you?"

Stacey laughed. "If she hadn't, half the town would have. Your little torrid moment didn't exactly go unnoticed." I didn't think it was possible for my cheeks to get any hotter. "It sounded kind of nice, what has you so worked up about it anyway?"

I threw myself backward on the couch and covered my face with a cushion. "Ugh. It's so dumb."

"What? I can't hear you." Stacey tugged on the cushion, and I relented enough to let her pull it down past my mouth, but I held tight when she tried to get it away from me.

"I said, ugh, it's so dumb," I repeated in a tone of voice better suited to Aurie and her friends than to me. Stacey snickered.

"What's so dumb? That the whole town is gossiping about you?"

"No!" I cried. "Well, yes. But also... the whole kissing thing." The last half of the sentence came out in a whisper that Stacey had to lean forward to hear.

She sat up and laughed. "Cassie, you're a forty-year-old woman. You've done the kissing thing before."

I sighed and muttered into the cushion, "Max was only the second guy I ever kissed. And I don't think the first counted."

Stacey's eyes opened wide. "Did I just hear you say that you've only ever kissed Max before?"

I scootched myself a little higher and pushed the cushion down onto my lap. "There was one kid. In middle school. At a stupid spin-the-bottle party. He wiped his mouth after and told everyone I'd given him cooties. My mom wouldn't let me date in high school and, well, you know I met Max right after I got to college. So, no, I've never kissed anyone other than Max."

In the ten-plus years I'd known Stacey, I'd never seen her speechless before. She kept leaning forward to look at me and then sitting back up, blinking and tilting her head.

"I know. I know. It's bad. Stace, what if I... don't remember how?" I muttered the last few words, but if her giggles were anything to go by, she hadn't missed a word I'd said.

"Would you..." she said, gasping for breath between snorts of laughter, "like to practice on a cushion? Or maybe on a mirror?"

Seeing the look on my face, she quickly set her glass down on the coffee table and grabbed a cushion to protect herself as mine came flying at her.

"I think I can remember how to kiss, you goof." I shook my head. "But what if... you know." I glanced down at my crotch and wiggled my eyebrows suggestively.

"Well, when a man and a woman love each other very, very much…" Stacey started, a mock-serious look on her face.

"I am going to hurt you," I threatened with a glare.

"Okay. Okay. I'm sorry." She took a deep breath and composed herself. "I'm sorry for laughing at your precarious situation."

"It is precarious! It has been a very long time since my… ah…. love garden has seen any… uh action." My face heated up again. "I can't even bring myself to talk about it! That's how bad things are!"

Stacey struggled for a moment but managed to reign in her laughter and school the massive grin threatening to split her face in half. "I'm going to assume that Max was your… one and only?"

"Yes! What kind of woman do you take me for?" I asked, indignation making my voice squeaky. Max and I hadn't always been stupid in love with each other, but it had never occurred to me to stray. I'd taken my vows to heart.

"Oh, gimme a break, you know I wasn't insinuating you're a hussy. I was just asking!"

"Thank you," I replied feeling a lot like an indignant schoolmarm whose reputation had been questioned. "Yes, Max was my one and only." My defensiveness vanished, and I slumped back down. "Ugh. This is ridiculous. I'm a forty-year-old mother and I'm nervous about going on a date because the guy might put the moves on me. I am ridiculous."

"No!" Stacey threw her arms around me and pulled me against her. "You are not ridiculous! You've had one guy in your life, and he treated you terribly! Of course, you're nervous about going on a date!"

"Maybe I should just cancel." Just saying the words made me feel a million tons lighter. I could stay home and chill on the couch with Stacey and Aurie. We could order pizza and watch chick flicks until it was way past our bedtime. And wine! We could have wine! And I wouldn't have to shave, or get dressed up, or worry about acting normal in public...

"You are NOT canceling! Are you insane?" Stacey's indignant reply cut into my daydream of the perfect Saturday evening. "Have you seen that man? If you don't go out with him, I will! It's hard not to wonder what he keeps under that uniform of his." Her grin said she had a good idea of what he kept under there, and she was a big fan.

"Hands off, woman," I growled, and we both laughed at the intensity of my reaction. "Okay then, I guess I'm going on this date."

"Heck yeah, you are! And you're going to love every darn minute of it!" Stacey crowed.

Time would be the judge of that, but the knot in the pit of my stomach wasn't encouraging.

SIX

I t wasn't that I didn't want to date Sam. It was more that I wanted to speed past the unpleasantness of the first date and the getting-to-know-you part of the relationship. I wanted to skip to the part where we were comfortable around each other and already knew everything we needed to know about each other.

What if he decided he didn't like me after all? What if he thought I was boring? What if...

All right, Cassie. Time to get out of bed and get a grip. You are a middle-aged woman with plenty of experience under her belt. Sure, it was with one guy, but still. You're not a blushing schoolgirl. You're an accomplished woman who runs her own business and who's rocking the single-parent thing... And who's still got it!

My little mental pep talk finally slowed the stream of potential date disasters rushing through my brain, though the thought of me still having 'it' made me snicker. Running a bakery had seriously cut into my already sporadic exercise routine while also giving me an endless supply of snacks and treats. I was a lot more woman than I'd been when I'd last gone on a first date.

Chuckling at the mental image of attempting to shimmy my more mature body into the tube top I'd worn the day I'd met Max, I rolled out of bed and hunted around for my slippers. It would make an impression for sure, but maybe not the impression I was hoping for.

Not that I knew what to wear or had given it much thought. A fleeting moment of panic made me freeze. Did I have anything date appropriate in my closet? No doubt, Stacey would be adamant that no, I did not have anything acceptable in my closet to wear on a fun night about town. To be fair, she probably thought I had nothing in my closet I should *ever* wear, but she could pry my flannels and comfy jeans out of my cold dead hands. I'd waited too long to be allowed to wear what I wanted to let anyone else dictate what was acceptable or not.

If Sam didn't like me in my trademark duds, it was going to be a short date. There was no way I had time to go shopping between now and the time he said he'd pick me up.

The smell of rotten milk hit me halfway down the stairs, and I gagged. Stuffing my nose and mouth into the crook of my arm, I stumbled into the commercial kitchen, my eyes watering from the stench. It was a good thing I still hadn't eaten any breakfast because there was no way I would have kept it down.

"I don't know what's going on!" Christina cried in lieu of good morning. "It's been getting progressively worse since I got here."

My eyes followed her glance around the room. Nothing looked out of place, but the smell increased as I stepped into the room. Doing my best to suppress my gag reflex, I forced myself to walk toward the worst of it.

The pantry. Not the walk-in fridge, not the freezer. The smell was coming from the pantry. I braced myself and when I tugged the door open, the noxious cloud of fumes that rolled out over me almost knocked me over.

"Oh... oh..."

My face must have turned an interesting shade of green because Christina had the backdoor open before I got there. Nothing had ever smelled as delicious as the sweet, fresh-smelling garden air I couldn't stop gulping down. It took more than a few breaths before I was able to stand straight without worrying my stomach was going to turn itself inside out. When I was relatively sure I wasn't going to throw up, I glanced over at Christina who looked more than a little green around the gills herself.

"What the heck, Christina? What possessed you to put the dairy order in the pantry and not the fridge? And why are all the milk bottles open? Do you have any idea what that order costs me every week?"

Her eyes widened and she shook her head. "I didn't! I swear! I know I put everything in the fridge. I'm not an idiot, Cassie, I know milk goes in the fridge and not the pantry! And even if I had put the order there, dairy doesn't spoil that fast!"

"Well, how do you explain that stench? You must have done something wrong." I was able to bite back a frustrated scream, but my tone of voice still made her flinch. It wasn't like me to pull the boss card, I much preferred it when we all worked as a team, but two epic disasters in as many days were pushing me to the brink.

"I... I don't know." Christina shook her head and held her hands up defensively. "All I know is that I put everything away where it belonged before I left yesterday afternoon."

"I'm sorry, but that doesn't make any sense. Are you suggesting I came down in the night and intentionally moved my expensive order of milk, cream, and butter into the freaking pantry? Then opened all of the bottles of milk and cream?" I threw my hands in the air and huffed a frustrated sigh.

"I didn't say that!" Christina snapped, her usually calm and sweet voice giving way to frustration. "I just said I'm not the one who did!"

"Just like you're not the one who broke the faucet yesterday?" The words slipped out before I could stop them. I slapped a hand across my mouth and stared wide-eyed as Christina's face turned red with anger.

"You think I broke the faucet?"

I wanted to stop, I really did, but my frustration boiled over. We'd lost so much time and money yesterday, and losing an entire dairy order was an even bigger blow. Not to forget, it was Saturday. There was no way I'd get the farmer to deliver a new order over the weekend. "I don't know what I think, Christina! All I know is that you were the only one in the kitchen when it exploded yesterday, and you were the only one in the kitchen when the dairy order was delivered. What am I supposed to think?"

She stared at me; her eyes colder than I'd ever seen them. A muscle alongside her jaw ticked ominously. "I don't know, Cassie. Maybe you could think 'oh, that Christina, she works so hard for me, making me bread that customers rave about. I know she'd never do anything to sabotage my business.' Or 'wow, what a streak of bad luck we're having, I should check to see how my loyal assistant is handling it.' Or maybe even 'I bet Christina is bummed her brother is leaving, I should try to be nice to her today.'"

"Or maybe I could think that you've been distracted because Raph is leaving? And that's why everything is going to pot?" Again, the words came out unbidden, and I couldn't do anything to call them back.

Christina blinked a few times, her lips pressed into a tight line. She lifted her chin and reached behind her to untie her apron. She slipped it over her head and dropped it at my feet. "You know what? I don't have to take this. Enjoy baking the bread by yourself today."

She was halfway to the back gate before my mouth unfroze. "Christina! Wait! Come back!"

Without replying, she opened the gate and walked through it before letting it slam loudly behind her.

The sun wasn't even up, how was I already asking myself if the day could get any worse?

SEVEN

Originally, I'd hired Christina to help me in the kitchen so the entirety of the prep and cooking didn't rest solely on my shoulders. Within days of her arrival, though, it had become apparent that her strength lay in baking bread. It was with unmitigated relief, that I had handed over everything to do with bread and hadn't looked back.

It wasn't that I couldn't bake bread, it was that I didn't enjoy it and my lack of enthusiasm could be tasted in the end product. At the same time, if I didn't sell bread two days in a row, customers were going to start to rebel.

Christina ignored the two texts I sent begging her to please come back, and the one call I attempted went straight to voicemail. She'd either turned off her phone or she was screening my calls. The result was the same. It was the crack of dawn, I had mountains of pastries and bread loaves to bake, and I was alone in a kitchen that smelled like death. No, scratch that, that smelled worse than death.

What had possessed me to tear into her like that? Her presence at both disasters had been purely coincidental, right? It had to have been. Christina didn't have a vindictive bone in her body. Plus, it was painfully obvious there were easier ways to disrupt my life, if that had even been the goal.

With my heart in my throat, I pulled my phone out of my back pocket and started typing a series of texts to Stacey. Fingers crossed she hadn't silenced her phone for the night.

SOS.
Need help in kitchen.
Stat.
Please.
Begging.

    WTF, Cass. It's 5am.

I know. I know. But it's really an emergency.

    OMG. Are you ok? Are you hurt?

Not that kind of emergency. Can you please just come down?

The lack of reply either meant she'd fallen back asleep or she was on her way down. I prayed for the latter as I threw open the pantry door and started hauling the spoiled goods out the back door.

"Sweet heavens to Betsy, what is that smell?" Stacey stepped into the room and covered her nose and mouth with her arm. "Can't you..." she waved her free arm around the air.

"Use my magic to clear the air?" I scowled at her. "You don't think I tried that?" My magic had worked about as well as it had the day before, but I was too panicked to spare the issue any attention. "Can you just please help me?" I gestured in the direction of the remaining crate of milk cartons with my chin and hurried outside with the last box of cheese and butter.

The cheese and butter could possibly be salvaged, but I couldn't take the risk of poisoning my customers. As much as it pained me, it was safer to throw out everything.

Stacey dropped the last box next to the three already outside and stepped away to gulp down some fresh air. Bit by bit the green tinge of her face faded, and she looked more like herself. "Can we please make some coffee before you tell me what's going on?"

"I can probably rustle you up something resembling coffee," I replied, intending it to come out as a joke, but Stacey must have remembered my iffy coffee-making skills because she winced and then shrugged.

"Eh, if it has caffeine in it, I'll take it."

The air in the kitchen was somewhat improved by the removal of the offending dairy products. It still wasn't great, so I left the door open and threw open as many windows as I could. The freezing cold air did nothing to improve my mood.

"Ready to catch me up?" Stacey asked, taking the mug of brewed coffee I handed her and hugging it to her chest for warmth.

"The long and short of it is that I was mean to Christina, so she left in a huff leaving me to make everything myself. Oh, and my dairy order wasn't refrigerated so it spoiled."

Stacey turned down her lips and tilted her head with a 'welp' look on her face. "Oh-kay. And you need me for...?" she let her sentence trail off and looked pointedly at me.

"I need you to handle all the prep so I can focus on the cooking." I held my breath as I waited for her to react.

"Cassie," Stacey groaned. "You know I'm a terrible cook. I eat food, I don't make it."

"I know! I know! You don't have to bake anything, I swear! Just measure things out for me and get it all organized so *I* can bake it. Please? I wouldn't ask if I wasn't up the proverbial creek without a paddle."

Stacey begrudgingly agreed to lend a hand and, with her help, I managed to make most of our usual offerings. Radically paring down the menu to three different types of bread rather than the seven on the regular menu helped a ton.

By the time Crystal bustled into the store, humming a little ditty under her breath, I was a sweaty frazzled mess, but we had pastries and loaves of bread to sell.

"Crystal! Our hero! Coffee! Please!" Stacey begged, lifting her head from the counter. She'd let it drop there after taking the last of the pastries out of the oven and hadn't moved since.

Wrinkling up her nose, Crystal poked her head into the kitchen. "What is going on here? Where's Christina? And why does it smell so bad in here?"

The stool I dropped onto creaked ominously but didn't collapse under me even though I half expected it to. I propped up my elbows on the counter and lowered my head onto my hands.

"Sour milk and rancid butter. That's what you're smelling. And Cassie was mean to Christina, so she went home. I came down to help, so I have very much earned a double shot latte with extra foam." Stacey's recap was on the nose, so I just nodded without lifting my head.

"Cassie was mean to Christina?" Without looking up, I knew she was frowning. Out of the corner of my eye, I saw Stacey shrug. "And we haven't used magic to clear the air because...?"

"Tried. Didn't work," I mumbled into my hands.

"Well, can you maybe try in the shop? Otherwise, I don't think anyone is going to be able to stomach anything you've managed to pull together." The tension in Crystal's voice pulled me to my feet. I doubted it would work, but I was willing to give it a shot.

The smell wasn't nearly as bad in the storefront, but it was undeniably there. With a grimace, I screwed my face up in concentration and willed the air molecules around me into leaving via the open front door. As though my magic hadn't been misbehaving, the noxious air swirled out the door, letting in a deliciously stink-free breeze as it left.

"So much better, thank you." Crystal hurried to close the door. "Maybe you should try again in the kitchen. It's way too cold to keep all the windows open in there."

With the ovens going at full blast, Stacey and I had barely noticed the freezing air circulating in the kitchen, but now that we were done baking, the temperature was decreasing at an alarming rate.

I ducked back into the kitchen, screwed my face up, and focused on the air molecules, but instead of heeding my request as they had in the shop, they danced around me, refusing to go where I guided them. "It's not working," I said to Crystal who'd poked her head through the door to see what was happening. "I don't get it."

She stepped into the room and held out her hand. When the small fireball I knew she was attempting to conjure didn't appear, we looked at each other, twin frowns on our faces.

"Okay, that is really weird." Crystal popped back into the store and called back, "works fine in here. I'm texting Hattie. She might have an idea or two about why this is happening. While I'm at it, I'll text Amy and Juliette and let them know breakfast is cancelled."

"Do you think the kitchen is cursed?" Stacey asked, fear stretching her eyes wide. "Or maybe it's haunted?" She looked around the room as though looking for a ghost she might have failed to notice during the last two hours. We'd been moving fast, but not so fast we wouldn't have noticed a ghostly apparition.

"I don't know," Crystal replied.

My head snapped in her direction. "Wait, what?"

"Ugh, what is that smell?" Hattie asked, wrinkling her nose as she pushed through the swinging doors.

Crystal and Stacey filled her in while I looked around. It was driving me nuts that I still couldn't see anything out of place. It was like I'd seen something out of the corner of my eye, but I couldn't put my finger on it now that I was actively looking.

"Huh." Hattie didn't have strong elemental magic, but she had an affinity for earth magic which somehow helped her communicate with animals among other things. "I can't feel anything under my feet. It's like a void." She stepped into the bakery and came right back. "I feel it in there, but not in here. I guess I didn't notice yesterday because of all the water."

Her thoughtful look didn't leave her face as she walked around the room. We all watched her in silence until she stopped and pointed at the center of the worktable in the middle of the room. "I think that's the epicenter. There's something there that is causing a magical dead zone all around here." She made a circular gesture that encompassed most of the bakery. "The dead zone gets a little muted around the edges of the circle then vanishes a step beyond. Is there a way to access the middle of the island, Cassie?"

I shook my head and frowned, then dropped to my knees as a thought sprang to mind. To make clean-up easier, the industrial island sat on rolling casters, not straight on the floor. Anyone could have come in, moved it out of the way, placed something under it, and moved it back into place. It would have taken seconds at most.

An innocuous-looking little pouch sat on the ground, right under the center of the island. "There! What's that?" Everyone dropped to the ground and peered under the island.

"That is what is causing all this mischief," Hattie said in her usual matter-of-fact tone. "Do you have a long stick or a broom?"

"I can do you one better." In no time, I'd unlocked the four casters keeping the island in place and shifted the whole thing to the side. As one, we moved to encircle the little pouch. Now that it wasn't in the shadows anymore, I could see that it was a mauve mesh bag like you'd use to wrap a piece of jewelry, filled with twigs and stones. "Wait, isn't that one of the mesh bags Amy uses in her booth?" I looked up at Crystal with a frown.

"Yeah, but, I mean, she buys them in bulk, anyone can get them." The defensive edge to Crystal's tone came as a surprise. I hadn't been accusing anyone of anything, so why the need to be so defensive? My back twinged as I swooped down to scoop up the little bag.

"Stop! Don't touch it with your bare hands!" Hattie cautioned.

Gingerly, I picked it up using the corner of my apron to protect my hand. Holding it in front of my face, I peered at the contents of the bag. It was exactly what it looked like, a little bag of sticks and stones, and ew, were those bones? I scrunched up my face and looked closer. Yep, tiny little mouse bones.

"What the heck is it?" I asked, glancing at Hattie who appeared more than a little discombobulated.

"That is some very old magic. It's not something you see often around here." She replied, sounding more awed than usual.

"What should I do with it?" Now that I was holding the little bag, I could feel the malevolence it radiated and I wanted nothing more than to toss the whole thing in the trash and never think about it again. I doubted that was an option.

"Burn it," Hattie said, in a tone that brooked no argument.

"Crystal, can you do your thing?" I asked, turning to her.

She squinted a little and frowned before shaking her head. "No. My magic doesn't seem to be able to touch it."

"It can't. That's a magic-neutralizing hex bag," Hattie explained. "We're going to have to use more traditional methods." She plucked the little pouch out of my hand with a long pair of kitchen tongs she found on the drying rack and dropped it into the empty stainless-steel sink next to the one filled with dirty dishes. "Do you have one of those torch thingies for caramelizing sugar?"

"In the drawer to your right," I replied, gesturing to the center drawer next to her knee. She pulled out the little torch and without hesitation, turned it to high. The little pouch caught fire easily and burned brightly before flaring bright green for an instant and flaming out.

"Whoa. That was cool," Stacey said, peering over Hattie's shoulder.

"That's one way to put it." The tension had left Hattie's voice and her usual good humor was seeping back in. "Cass, give your magic a try."

Not expecting much, I focused on the air around me and twirled my arm in a spiral motion. As if nothing had ever been wrong, the air did what I asked of it. "It's fine. Totally back to normal."

"Great, maybe you could sweep the rest of the noxious fumes out of here before our first customers arrive, then," Crystal said, glancing at the clock.

I followed her gaze and swore. We had all of five minutes before our regulars would start demanding service. It only took two to clear the air and close all the windows. While I did that, Stacey, Crystal, and Hattie took all the baked goods and organized them in the display case. When the first customer rolled in, it was like nothing had ever happened. Except my nerves were shot, I was exhausted beyond belief, and I couldn't stop thinking about the charm.

I had a pretty good idea of *who* had placed it there, but the *why* was eluding me. Was the point to annoy me and make my life more difficult? Or did she have something bigger planned that I couldn't envision? Either way, if the rest of the day had more unpleasant surprises in store for me, there was no way I was going to make it all the way to my date without crying, screaming, or falling asleep in my coffee. Possibly all three, not necessarily in that order.

EIGHT

Getting Aurie out of bed on a weekend morning was usually a struggle, so I was surprised to find her up, dressed, and almost finished with breakfast when I snuck upstairs to check on her as soon as the opening rush lulled.

"You're up early!" I kept trying to banish my bad mood to the dark recesses of my brain, but I couldn't seem to shake it, so my comment came out with a little more edge than intended.

Aurie's smile faded a little. "Remember? I have to help Hattie winterize the rabbit hutches today?"

Right. She had told me, but in the chaos of the last two days, it had slipped my mind. "Oh. Yes. Sorry. I knew that." I forced a bright smile on my face, but she still looked wary.

"You okay, Mom? You're acting weird."

I dropped the smile and sighed. "I'm fine. Weird morning, but everything is copacetic now."

She frowned and tilted her head to look at me. "What's that mean?"

I chuckled. "It's old people speak for 'everything is fine.'" Arching my eyebrow, I pointed to her empty breakfast bowl on the coffee table, then the dishwasher before opening the freezer to find something to defrost for dinner without waiting to see the eye roll I knew was coming.

"Oh. Well, if everything is coceptic, why do you seem so upset?" she asked, dropping her bowl and spoon into the sink with a clatter.

I debated arguing with her about putting it in the dishwasher and decided it wasn't worth the effort. "Copacetic, and it's nothing important."

"You never let me get away with not telling you," she said, scowling.

"It's really no big deal, I promise." I grasped at straws for a way to change the subject. After her close brush with death, she was leery about magic, and I didn't want to exacerbate her misgivings. She needed to feel safe so she could get over what had happened, not worry that more magic was going to hurt one of us. "Do you have your hat and gloves? It's snowing again."

My bad mood flared back to life when she glanced away and shifted her feet. "You didn't? Seriously Aurie? You lost another hat?" She shook her head, but still didn't meet my gaze. "Your gloves? Are you kidding me? That's three pairs just this month! You have got to start being more careful with your things!" I knew my frustration wasn't entirely related to the lost gloves, but I couldn't keep it in check. "I guess it's a good thing your field trip was canceled. There's no way I can run out and get you another pair this weekend."

Aurie perked up. "It's not canceled anymore! Grandad emailed the teacher and offered to drive the school bus! She said that could work since he has a truck driving license!" She bounced on her toes, my rant about her gloves entirely forgotten. "It's going to be so fun. My friends are going to be so jealous my grandad is the driver! Think he'll let me sit on his lap while he drives?"

My brain had stopped following her flow of words when she'd announced my father would be driving the bus, so it took me a moment to realize she'd asked a question.

"What? No. You can't sit on his lap. Have you lost your mind?"

She shrugged like it didn't matter one way or another. "Whatever. It's still cool. And now we get to go." She did a little happy dance as she bounced toward the door and turned back abruptly. "I'm sorry about the gloves, Mom. I promise I'll try harder to keep track of my things."

Concern over my father driving a school bus of rowdy children on icy streets had pushed all thoughts of missing winter gear right out of my head but being reminded of it made my irritation flare back to life. She was halfway down the stairs before I could voice further admonitions to be more careful.

Instead of chasing after her, I pulled out my phone and texted my father.

Please tell me Aurie is kidding and you didn't offer to drive her class to Walden Pond.

Why on earth would I tell you that when it isn't true?

What are you thinking? Seriously. Do you have any idea what you've gotten yourself into?

Oh, please. I've driven big rigs through historic blizzards.
Driving a school bus is going to be a piece of cake.
Plus, it's not like I had anything better to do.

Guilt layered itself on top of my growing frustration. I knew he was bored, but this seemed like such a reckless way to combat that. My thumbs hovered over the keyboard until I accepted that nothing I said would convince him to change his mind. We were still getting to know each other, but I'd inherited my pig-headedness from him and I knew that if I pushed, he'd dig his heels in just for the satisfaction of fighting me.

My head ached from the tension gripping my neck. I needed an hour-long soak in a bubble bath with an over-sized glass of wine, but I had a full day of work waiting for me. I added convincing my father to bow out of his asinine commitment and finding time to get Aurie some new gloves to my ever-growing to-do list and headed back down the stairs. With any luck, the lull had lasted long enough for Crystal to brew me a massive latte.

NINE

Despite my best efforts, and a series of magic-laced lattes whipped up throughout the morning by Crystal, I couldn't shake the skin-crawling heaviness weighing me down. Every time I started to perk up, I remembered the evil magic that had been placed in the middle of my kitchen, and my mood crashed back down into the dumps.

"I just can't wrap my brain around the purpose of placing that thing there," I said to Crystal for the umpteenth time. "Why can't she just let me be? I'm a good person just trying to make people's lives better with yummy pastries and a cozy place to hang out for a while. I'm not a threat! Why can't she see that?"

"Well, for starters, you don't know for a fact that it was her," Crystal said, not for the first time. "And if it was, you know full well why she can't."

"But you have to admit it's insane behavior, right?" I knew I was beating a dead horse, but the prickly feeling that someone was staring at me had been making the skin on the back of my neck crawl since we'd found the damn thing, and I kept having to glance over my shoulder to make sure no one was behind me. I doubted Margie was actively spying on me, but for all I knew, she'd hidden other hex bags around the bakery or even in my house. "I just feel so violated."

"I know, Cassie." Crystal was doing her best to be patient and understanding, but I could tell my behavior was starting to grate on her nerves. It didn't help that we'd had a constant stream of customers since we'd opened, and I was so distracted she was having to work twice as hard. "We will give the place a thorough once over after we close, but right now, we have more pressing matters." Another large party came in and she groaned. "Could you *please* text Christina again and beg her to come help?"

"I think she's turned off her phone. She hasn't answered any of my texts." Guilt gnawed at my belly, partly because I wasn't sure the morning would play out differently if I had to do it over again. Someone had royally messed up and Christina was the only person who'd been in the kitchen at the time of the incident. As much as I loved my assistant, a mistake of that caliber was still infuriating.

Plastering a smile on my face, I turned to the next customer in line.

"Good morning! What can I get started for you?" I asked the young brunette beaming at me.

"I'm here to pick up the cake my mother ordered last week. I can't wait to see how it turned out." As she clapped her hands together with excitement, I froze. Was it possible I'd forgotten a special order in the chaos? No, everything had only gone to pot yesterday. If I'd had an order on the books for today, I would have started working on it long before the faucet exploded.

"Crystal!" I hissed out of the corner of my mouth. "This young woman is here for her cake order. Do you know anything about it?" I stared at her, my eyes as wide as I could make them.

Crystal frowned and shook her head. "We didn't have any special orders for today."

"That's what I thought." A pit formed in my stomach, but I did my best to smile at the customer whose cheerful expression was quickly giving way to a worried frown. "I'm so sorry, but are you sure your mother asked for it to be made today?"

The customer's smile dimmed further. "Of course, I'm sure. It's for their 50th anniversary party. She's been married 50 years, she wouldn't get the date wrong. She said she came in here last week and placed the order in person. I remember it clearly because she was so excited to be getting a cake from the magic wand bakery."

Shaking my head, I glanced at Crystal whose face had blanched as the girl spoke. "I am so sorry. I..." her eyes rolled wildly in my direction. "I'm sorry. I must have forgotten to tell you. I..." She turned back to the customer who looked equally horrified.

"No. You don't understand. My mother is going to lose her mind. She's been planning this party for months. The entire dessert table is designed around the cake. We can't *not* have a cake!" Her anguish tasted like hot coals, and it was all I could do to resist reaching over the counter to pull her into my arms.

I smiled as reassuringly as possible. "Everything is going to be okay. Crystal, did you take any notes when the order was placed?"

Crystal stopped flipping through the pages of the special order book and shook her head. "I'm sorry! I know I wrote down what was ordered, but it was on a scrap piece of paper. I was going to add it to the book, and I must have forgotten."

I took a deep breath to suppress the scream building up in my chest and smiled as broadly as possible at the customer whose lower lip was starting to quiver. "It's okay.

Everything is going to be okay," I repeated more to appease myself than our young customer. "What can you tell me about the party? I'm sure I can make something work. It might not be exactly the cake your mother ordered, but I can promise it'll be delicious."

She blinked away a tear and followed me to the end of the counter while Crystal resumed taking care of the growing line of customers. As the young woman described the color scheme of the party and told me a little about her parents, Crystal snuck covert looks at us, but I couldn't bring myself to meet her eye. If I did, I was terrified my anger would boil over, and I wouldn't be able to hold back from telling her exactly how I felt.

"Okay, honey, I think I can make something work. On the house, of course. I have no idea what happened, but I can assure you, this isn't how we usually operate. This kind of mistake is inexcusable." I glanced toward Crystal who blushed without meeting my gaze. "Why don't you have a seat, and I'll whip something up in no time. Tell my partner over there what you'd like to drink, and she'll take care of you."

As I brushed past Crystal, she grabbed my arm. "Cassie, I know I messed up, but you cannot leave me to handle this crowd on my own."

I shook my arm loose. "What exactly do you want me to do? Not make that poor kid a cake? Did you see the look on her face?" I snapped.

Crystal threw her hands in the air. "Ugh. I don't know! But I can't be here alone! Look at that!" She gestured to the line of customers snaking around the room.

"Fine. I'll text Stacey and have her come help you. I can even see if my dad is around." She heaved a sigh of relief, and I narrowed my eyes at her. "But you and I are not done talking about this. I cannot *believe* you didn't write down that order," I hissed.

"I know! I know! I can't believe it either. Amy walked in right after the woman left, and I guess I let myself get distracted."

"Of course, it's about Amy. It's always about Amy. I swear, ever since we first met her..." I bit my tongue and took a deep breath.

Crystal reared back and crossed her arms defensively. "Go on, please. Ever since we first met her...?"

"Let's not get into it right now. We can talk later." I started to turn away and she grabbed my arm again.

"Oh, no. I think I want you to finish that sentence right now." Her nostrils flared, and I hesitated. The line was only getting longer, and we had a large audience of restless hungry people clutching phones in their hands. A video of the two of us going at it behind the counter wasn't exactly the kind of publicity I wanted. I would have walked away, but I snapped when I spied the young cake customer, frantically typing on her device, tears running down her face.

"Fine! Ever since Amy arrived on the scene, you've been distracted. I hate to say it, but I don't think you're pulling your weight around here."

Crystal gasped and clutched her chest. "Are you kidding me? I'm here every single day. I do every little thing you ask of me! I even come when I'm not supposed to be working when you ask! And when I'm not here, I'm probably working on marketing and social media. How dare you say I'm not pulling my weight! I'm here more often than you!"

My face flamed, and I suddenly wanted to be anywhere but there. Crystal reached behind her and started tugging at her apron strings. Blind panic made the world around me lurch. If she walked out, I was well and truly sunk.

Setting aside my anger about the missing order, I threw myself on her mercy. "Stop, please stop. I'm sorry! I'm not myself today. I didn't mean a word of what I said. I'm sorry. Of course, you pull your weight. I would be lost without you." My frantic torrent of words barely made any sense as they tumbled out, but at least Crystal had stopped untying her apron and was looking at me with an unreadable expression.

"And...?" she prompted.

"And... and..." I scrambled, not sure what she wanted to hear. "You're amazing and your coffee is legendary, and you're gorgeous and funny and awesome all around."

Crystal chuckled. "Thanks, but that's not what I was getting at. Amy?"

"Oh! Right, sorry. Amy is not a distraction. She's gorgeous and funny and awesome too, and I'm beyond glad the two of you are finally together."

Mollified, she re-tied her apron and cocked her head. "That'll do. For now."

Relief made me giddy and I grabbed the counter to stay standing. "Are we good?"

Crystal shrugged; her expression still reserved. "We're okay. As long as you get Stacey and Hugh down here pronto. I have hungry customers to serve. I'll text Amy to see if she can come pitch in."

With my stomach lodged in my throat, I hurried to the kitchen. I needed to get a grip before I alienated all my friends and coworkers and ruined everything I'd fought so hard to get. My whole life was starting to feel like a house of cards on the verge of collapsing, and I was the one about to knock it over.

We kept a few sparsely decorated cakes in the large walk-in freezer just in case a customer needed one for a spur-of-the-moment celebration. Our young customer hadn't known what flavors her mother had ordered, so I pulled out a small vanilla cream, a medium carrot cake, and a large chocolate cake and in minutes had all three stacked in a neat tower.

Stacey sauntered into the room as I started piping frosting onto the top tier. "How exactly do you keep this place running when I'm in the city?" she teased on her way to grab an apron from the hook beside the swinging door.

When I didn't reply, because I couldn't without letting loose a waterfall of tears, she turned and frowned.

"Aw, babe. Crummy day, eh?"

A bitter chuckle burst out of me dislodging the tight wad of emotions lodged in my throat. "You could say that."

"Is there anything I can do beyond help out in the shop?"

I shrugged, knowing full well I'd dug myself into this hole and I was going to have to dig myself out. "Trust me, rescuing Crystal is plenty."

She pushed the swinging door open and glanced back at me. "How about we go shopping after the bakery closes? Get you something cute for your date?"

My heart was already resting at the bottom of the pit in my stomach, but somehow her words made it sink further. I'd forgotten about the date. The kitchen was a disaster because I hadn't had time to clean after the morning baking frenzy, and if Christina stayed away for the rest of the day, I had all of tomorrow's prep to handle on my own on top of getting the place back in some sort of acceptable order. There was no way I had time to go shopping. Heck, I wasn't even sure I had time to go on the date.

Stacey took one look at the silent tears her words had unleashed and backtracked. "Let's get through this morning and we'll reassess." I managed a thin smile in reply. "Don't give up! You've got this."

Her encouragement lifted my spirits enough to face the plainly decorated cake in front of me without letting lose another round of tears. Throwing my shoulders back, I picked up a piping bag filled with frosting and got to work. The only way out of this disaster of a day was through, and the least I could do was make sure the young woman waiting for this cake had something beautiful to show for her ordeal.

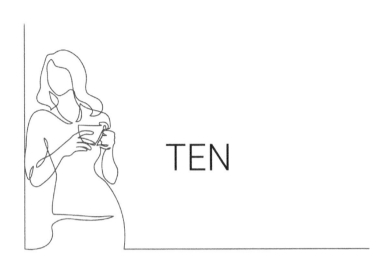

TEN

Decorating the 50th Anniversary cake had taken a little longer than expected. By the time I deemed it ready to box up Stacey, Crystal, and my father had fallen into a good rhythm and shooed me back into the kitchen.

I'd tried not to take it personally and failed, though I didn't blame them for not wanting to be around me. *I* didn't want to be around me.

Maybe I wasn't cut out for this life. If all it took to derail me were a few kitchen disasters and a magical hex bag, maybe this wasn't the place for me. To make up for the money I'd lost over the faucet situation and replacing the dairy order I was going to have to take on a few extra catering events, which meant I was going to have to rely on my dad to take care of Aurie and Crystal to take care of the bakery. And as Crystal had pointed out, it wasn't like she wasn't already working her butt off.

I swiped away a tear moments before it dropped into the dough I was gathering and sniffed. It was all just too much. I was insane to have thought running a bakery and raising Aurie at the same time was sustainable long-term.

When the swinging doors squeaked, it took me a moment to pull myself out of my dark thoughts and notice Stacey, Crystal, and miraculously, Christina staring at me from the other side of the island.

"What are you all doing here? Who's watching the bakery?" I asked, blinking the outside world into focus.

"Hon? It's after three. The bakery has been closed for a while," Crystal said, pointing at the large clock on the wall.

I looked at the rows of croissants in front of me and the rows of tartlets beyond them and couldn't remember making any of them. My friends were all staring at me with matching worried frowns. "I guess I lost track of time." Was it possible I'd been so wrapped up in my thoughts I had done most of the prep without realizing it? The full racks of pastries proofing beside me, and the tower of clean dishes seemed to indicate that was exactly what had happened. "Oh, that's not good." The noise in my head increased as I took in the sheer amount of work I'd done and realized I hadn't been monitoring my mental shields while doing it. I looked up at my friends, my bottom lip caught between my teeth, and shook my head.

"That's not good," Crystal echoed me.

"What?" Stacey asked, looking around the pristine kitchen. "You did great!"

Christina groaned. "Ugh. Who wants to be the guiney pig?"

"What's wrong?" Stacey asked again, her voice a little louder.

I leaned forward and let my head drop onto the cool work counter. "I wouldn't if I were any of you. I was having some pretty dark thoughts. We should probably throw it all out." Tears welled in my eyes and overflowed, hitting the counter without a sound. Another debacle and no one to pin this one on other than me.

"Ohhhh" Stacey dragged out the vowel. "Crud." She'd been one of the earliest recipients of the baked goods my magic had leaked into before I even knew I was a witch. For the most part, the intent I baked into magical pastries didn't influence people in directions they weren't already leaning, but I also didn't want to ruin everyone's day with the food I'd prepared while moping.

"All right. That's it. This is an intervention." Crystal clapped her hands together. "Cassie? You need a break. Like yesterday." I raised my head and looked at her. She had to be kidding, right? The last thing I had time for was a break. "I know what you're going to say, so save it.

Christina and I are going to fix this." She waved at the mound of potentially magical pastries I'd prepared. "You and Stacey are going shopping and getting you dolled up for your date."

When I straightened up and opened my mouth to protest, she stared me down. "I said, stuff it. You haven't taken a break in weeks. You're unraveling. And we need you out of here. Plus, Sam would probably cry if you canceled on him, and no one wants to see that. So, before we change our minds and decide to hold grudges for your abysmal behavior this morning, get out of here." She took a threatening step toward me and growled in a way that seemed less playful than I assumed she intended.

Throwing my hands up in surrender, I gave in. "Fine. I'll go shopping. For an hour. Then I can come back and redo all this."

Crystal growled again, shaking her head. "No. You're going shopping. Then you're taking a long soapy bath. Then, you're getting all pretty and going. On. A. Date. This kitchen and the shop are out of bounds until tomorrow morning. Am I making myself clear?" Her expression softened. "We've got this. Trust me."

"But..." I glanced over at Christina, an apology on the tip of my tongue, but she shook her head before I could say a word.

"No buts," Christina said. "You need a break. We can start fresh tomorrow."

An intense wave of gratitude made my knees wobbly. "I guess we have to go shopping," I said to Stacey with a wry smile.

"It's a hard life, but somebody has to live it," she replied with a laugh, slipping her hand into the crook of my arm and tugging me toward the swinging doors.

ELEVEN

It was a good thing Stacey was both good at shopping and loved it, because whenever I came face to face with a rack of clothing, it was like my mind shut down.

"Here, try these on," she said, tossing a stack of jeans over the changing room door.

"What's wrong with the jeans I own?" I knew I sounded like a petulant child, but nothing made me feel worse about my body than trying on jeans.

"You bought those jeans at a thrift store. That's what's wrong with them. Who knows how many people have worn them before you. These jeans will make your butt look like a million dollars instead of saggy potato sacks."

Twisting around, I checked out my backside in the mirror and had to admit she might have a point. "But they're comfortable!"

"So are the ones I tossed you! Come on, what do you have to lose? I'll be right back. I saw some tops I think would be perfect for you."

"What do I have to lose? Oh, nothing but my last smidges of self-respect," I muttered, knowing full well she couldn't hear me.

With a sigh, I pulled the stack of jeans off the door and hung them up. I ignored the skinny jeans and unhooked a cute boot-cut pair with funky stitching around the seams and the back pockets. They slipped on and buttoned up easily, and when I turned around to see how they looked from the back, my jaw dropped. "Welp! I did not expect that!"

"Didn't expect what?" Stacey asked, tossing a few more things over the door.

"Uh...for my butt to look like this," I said, opening the door and turning around to show her.

"Oh! Nice! See? What did I say? Have you tried on the rest?"

"Do I really need to?" I asked, gesturing to my backside.

Stacey laughed. "Fine, you can get these, but you also have to try on a pair of skinny jeans."

"Do I have to?" I whined. "Skinny jeans make my butt look big."

"First of all, some people like a nice round ass. Second of all, your butt isn't big, it's perfectly proportioned to your body. Third, that's a terrible, outdated notion and yes, you have to." She pointed to the darkest of the skinny jeans she'd brought. "Hop to it."

Grumbling the whole time, I reluctantly peeled off the bootcut jeans and unhooked the skinny pair. In Stacey's defense, they were the softest pair of jeans I'd ever touched and slipping into them was like sliding into a bucket of warm moon sand. "Oh, hello. Come to mama," I murmured.

Stacey laughed on the other side of the door.

Before I finished buttoning them up, I spun around and stood there gaping like an idiot.

"So? Do they fit?" Stacey asked, banging on the door.

"Uh-huh." I fumbled for the latch without taking my eyes off the mirror. "Why didn't anyone tell me I could look like this in jeans?" I demanded.

"We did. You're just a little pig-headed at times."

"Please tell me these don't cost as much as a car." Not that it mattered. These jeans were coming home with me even if I had to sell a kidney to afford them.

"I wouldn't do that to you! They're reasonably priced and they're on sale. Anyway, they're on me. Birthday present."

I narrowed my eyes at her. "My birthday was over six months ago and you know it."

"Fine, it's an advance on your next birthday," she said, waving off my protest.

"You can't buy me jeans. That's weird," I protested.

"No, it's not. And it's the least I can do." She glanced away, but I saw the tears in the corners of her eyes.

"What are you talking about? Why are you upset?"

"Not upset. Grateful. I am so stinkin' happy here and it's all thanks to you. If it hadn't been for your scones, I would never have walked away from Dylan and I would never have dared apply for this job. It's like I was stuck, and you freed me. So, if I want to buy you a pair of jeans to say thank you, you're going to let me. Okay?" She swiped angrily at the tears flowing down her face and I pulled her into a tight hug.

"If you feel that strongly, you can buy me both pairs, okay?"

She laughed and pushed me away. "It's not that I don't love you, but you're just wearing a bra and I doubt the security camera operator needs any more wet dream fodder than he already gets."

"Eeps!" I squealed, grabbing the slinky top she handed me and looking around for cameras.

"I'm kidding. I think." She glanced around, not looking as sure as she sounded.

The top she'd handed me was so unlike anything I'd ever worn, I gave her a dubious look.

"Are we really doing this again?" She rolled her eyes. "Just try it on."

I slipped the blue silky material over my head and marveled at the way it slithered down my torso and came to rest on my hips. Artful folds flowed down my front, somehow both highlighting my chest and hiding my less appealing muffin top. "Oh. Wow."

"Yes!" Stacey crowed. "Now all you need is a kick-ass pair of shoes and you're ready to slay tonight." I opened my mouth to protest, and she glared at me until I snapped it shut.

The protest would have been a knee-jerk reaction anyway. I hadn't felt this sexy in a very, very long time, and as much as I hated to admit it, I couldn't wait to see how a pair of heels would tie the whole look together.

"You okay? You've been strangely silent since we left the shoe department." Stacey put down her mug and shot me a worried look.

After buying the least practical and most gorgeous pair of strappy heels I had ever tried on let alone held, Stacey had taken pity on me and called it a day on the shopping spree. Before hitting the shoe department, she'd coerced me into getting both pairs of jeans (one of which she'd paid for) and three flowy, silky tops in various colors and cuts. I doubted I'd ever have a chance to wear them, but even if she hadn't insisted, I didn't think I could have put them back on the rack. They made me feel pretty and soft.

I blinked a few times and shook my head to clear it. "Sorry. I was a million miles away." We'd found a cute coffee shop nearby and stopped in for some much-needed sustenance. Being on the customer side of the counter was a little disorienting.

"Where did you go?" she asked, before taking a sip of her latte.

"He always made me feel fat," I said, looking away.

"Who? Max?" She made a face as if his name left a bad taste in her mouth.

"Yeah. He never actually came out and said so, but I could see it in his eyes every time I tried to wear something a little more form-fitting than usual. And for years I believed him. But you know what I saw in that mirror today?" Stacey raised an eyebrow and let me continue without interrupting. "I saw a gorgeous ass. I saw a sexy woman! How I've lost weight while working in a bakery is beyond me. But the proof was right there in front of me. Plain as day!" Picturing myself in that mirror made me blush.

Stacey snorted so hard latte foam flew across the table. She looked at me and shook her head, laughing to herself.

"What? What's so funny?"

"You're funny," she replied.

"No, I'm not. Tell me what made you laugh?"

"Hon, you haven't lost any weight since you left Georgia." She leaned to the side and looked me up and down. "If anything, I'd say you've put on a few pounds." My head snapped up and I stared at her, mouth open. "Oh, can it. They're good pounds. They look good on you. You finally have a little meat on your bones."

I snapped my mouth shut and blinked at her. "What are you talking about?"

"You look alive and healthy. More importantly, you look happy, like someone who's embraced life. It looks good on you." Her smile held a hint of mischief. "You look like the kind of woman who would chew Max up and spit him out. He never thought you were overweight, he just didn't like you looking confident."

Her last sentence landed with as much force as a one-two punch from a prizefighter and the truth of her words left me feeling dizzy and strangely weightless.

"That is one hundred percent true." I slumped back in my chair, my body and my arms suddenly too heavy for me to stay upright.

Stacey met my gaze and a small sad smile tugged at the corner of her lips. "Sorry. That was a lot of truth to throw at you all at once."

I shook my head. "No. It was the right amount of truth. You're so right. I can't believe I never saw it. It wasn't just clothing. It was everything that brought me joy or made me feel accomplished. He hated it all. I always thought it was because it took time away from our family, but that wasn't it at all."

She squeezed her lips together and shook her head slowly from side to side. "Nope. That wasn't it."

"Well...crud." I reached for my mug and held it against my chest. "That is a lot to process." A wave of fear sent a shiver down my back. "What if..." I couldn't bring myself to say the words out loud.

"Don't even go there," Stacey said, waving her hands in front of her. "Nope. Sam and Max are not the same person. Has Sam ever looked like he minds that you work or that you have a fulfilling life?" I shook my head. "I've seen that man look at you. He likes what he sees. He's not going to want you to change. Well..."

My heart sank. I knew it was too good to be true. "What?"

"He is going to wish you wore more sexy clothing after he sees you in that outfit tonight." Her eyes sparkled with mischief. "*Vavavoom*! If you know what I mean."

My face heated up and I squirmed in my seat. I knew all too well what she meant. "Maybe it's too much for a first date. I should have picked something more demure."

"Ha!" Stacey laughed. "The outfit we picked isn't exactly showgirl material. It's perfectly appropriate for a first date. Trust me. Just because you look sexy as hell in it doesn't make it racy."

I wasn't convinced, but also, I really wanted to wear my snazzy new jeans and pretty new blouse, even if thinking about Sam seeing me in the outfit was doing weird things to my nether regions. I squirmed a little more in my seat and changed the subject.

"With my luck, some epic catastrophe will either force me to cancel the date or to abort it mid-way." And just like that, the weight of the last few days came crashing back down on my shoulders. "Going out in the first place is ridiculous. I should stay home and brainstorm how I'm going to make back all that money and try to figure out who snuck that hex bag into my kitchen in the first place. Plus, I really screwed the pooch with Christina this morning. I should make time to apologize properly. And Crystal... that was bad too. Though not writing down an order was really messed up..."

"Woah!" Stacey held up her hands. "Slow that roll. Sit up and repeat after me, 'I am allowed to go out and have fun.'"

"I'm not doing that." I rolled my eyes at her.

"'I am allowed to have fun.' Say it." She pinned me with a stare.

"Ugh. Fine." I sat up and repeated, "I am allowed to have fun."

"Good. Good. Now this. 'The world will not stop turning if I don't think about work, my employees, or my family for an evening.'" She quirked an eyebrow and fixed her gaze on me.

"I do not think the world will stop turning if I don't do those things. And also, Crystal is my partner, not my employee." Stacey's expression didn't waver, and I gave in. "You're ridiculous. The world will not stop turning if I... whatever you said. Happy?"

"It was a pretty poor repetition, but I'll take it. For crying out loud, Cassie, you are allowed to do something just for you for one evening! I promise everything will be fine."

"And what if someone sneaks another hex bag into the house and something horrible happens when I'm not there?" I was being belligerent, but the fear making it hard to draw a full breath was real.

"If that happens, which it won't, I'll be there and your dad will be there. And Hattie is four feet away. And Juliette is a quick phone call away. Heck, *you*'ll be a quick phone call away. But also, did I mention nothing is going to happen?"

"You don't know that for sure," I said, but a little of the pressure on my chest had eased up making it easier to draw breath.

"No, I don't, but I think we can roll with whatever comes our way. And can we please stop pretending we don't know who left that thing in your kitchen?"

"I mean, I thought I knew, but everyone seems so convinced that I'm wrong. And what if I am? Last thing I want is to rile Margie up any further. That woman already hates me so much, if I start slandering her right and left, that's not going to get better any time soon," I said, slumping back into my seat and hating how defeated I sounded. "Maybe there's another witch in town who has it in for me."

"Come on, do you really think that?" Stacey's eyebrows were so high they were almost touching her hairline.

I shrugged. "I sure hope not! One nemesis is all I can handle at once. You know," I said, looking her in the eye, "I don't think I'd mind as much if everyone believed me when I tell them she's out to get me. But they all think I'm overexaggerating."

"Well, they can't exactly ignore the thing she planted in your kitchen."

"There's no proof it was her!" I threw my hands up in exasperation. "She's not the only powerful witch in town."

"But she is the only one who's openly declared war on you," Stacey said, tilting her head and gesturing with her coffee.

"Exactly! So why are you the only one who believes me?" My blood pressure was rising again and negating all the good the afternoon of shopping had done. Obsessing over Margie wasn't doing me any good so I might as well focus on something positive. "Let's go. I want to take a nice long shower before I get ready for my date so I can be nice and relaxed this evening."

"Now we're talking! One hot shower, coming up." Stacey dropped our mugs in the dirty dish bin by the trash and tucked her arm in mine. "Whatever happens tonight or with Margie in the coming days, I have a good feeling about what's in store for you."

"Oh, you do, do you?" I laughed.

She tapped the side of her nose and gave me a serious, knowing look. "The nose knows, Cassie. The nose knows."

TWELVE

"How do I look?" I twirled and kicked up my foot in front of the couch where my father, Aurie, and Stacey were settling in for an evening of binging TV and stuffing their faces with pizza and ice cream. A tiny part of me was a little jealous I wouldn't be indulging with them, but the rest of me was quivering with excitement and nerves over the impending evening.

I knew I looked good in my bootylicious new jeans and flowy blouse, but the way they hooted and whistled in reply to my question did wonder for my confidence.

"You look amazing, Mom. So different!" Aurie said.

"Uh, thank you? I think?" I replied, trying to take her compliment at face value and not read into it too much.

"You know what I mean," she said, blushing slightly.

"I do, sweetie. Thank you."

"Those jeans were worth every penny! Look at that ass! Whoot!" Stacey called from the corner of the couch. "That man is not going to know what hit him."

"I shouldn't even comment after that," my father shook his head in Stacey's direction, "but you look good. Tell Sam he'll answer to me if he acts like a lout."

It was my turn to roll my eyes. "Dad, while this might be my first date in well over 15 years, it's not my first date ever, and I'm not a little girl who needs protecting. You missed that train." The instant I saw pain flash in his eyes, I wished I could take back my harsh words.

"Speaking of that..." he started to say, but I interrupted him before he could get too far.

"Speaking of my first dates?"

"No," he said, tightening his lips. "Speaking of that tongue of yours. There's no way to say this nicely, but I don't know if you've noticed, but you've been a little..." he hesitated, searching for the right word, "let's say aggressive, recently. There's an edge to you that isn't usually there, and I'm a little worried you're starting to burn bridges you can't afford to burn."

His words burst my bubble of excited anticipation and set my teeth on edge. My stomach clenched and nausea rose in my throat when I glanced at Stacey and Aurie who were doing their best not to look at me. Traitors.

"Oh, you think I've been a little on edge?" The fact that he was right made this conversation a million times worse. I hated feeling like I was going to bite everyone's head off as soon as they opened their mouth. While Stacey and I had been out shopping, I'd been more relaxed than I had in days, but the instant we'd stepped back into the bakery, all the tension that had me so wound up had sprung back into place.

"I'm sure it has nothing to do with the fact that I have three mouths to feed and a roof to keep over everyone's head, and I'm the only one working my fingers to the bone to make it happen. Or that everything keeps going haywire in my bakery and no one seems to give a rat's patooty." I slammed my lips shut when I saw the devastated look on Aurie's face. "I'm sorry! I'm sorry! I don't know why that keeps happening. I don't really think those things.

"I love you. I love having you here, dad, and of course, I don't resent you, Aurie. You're my baby girl and I treasure getting to take care of you. I don't know why I keep having these outbursts. It's like I'm cursed or something." I blinked back hot tears that threatened to ruin my already imperfect make-up job.

"It's okay, babe. We all know you're under a lot of stress. You've been working too hard," Stacey said with a sad smile.

My father looked as perturbed as Aurie, but they both pretended they weren't hurt by my rant.

"It's okay, Mom. I know you love us. Stacey's right. You're just working too much."

I winced. The amount I worked was a huge point of contention between the two of us, but for once it didn't sound like she was resentful of my workload, just worried about me. Still, I noticed no one picked up on my comment about being cursed.

Maybe they're all right and you are working too hard. People don't go around cursing other people. That can't really be a thing. Though, by that logic, people don't go around leaving evil hex bags in other people's homes, so...

My spiraling thoughts were interrupted by a knock on the door to the outside landing. Before the building had grown to accommodate my father, anyone coming over to visit had to come in through the bakery. It made seeing people after hours a little challenging. Along with the added apartment above ours, the building had materialized a set of outdoor steps leading to our landing and up to my father's apartment, making it easier for visitors to stop by.

Spinning around to face the couch I hissed, "You're sure I look okay?"

Stacey grinned. "You look great. Go open the door."

Taking a deep breath, I spun toward the door and promptly caught my heel on the edge of the carpet. My hand just missed catching the armchair to my right, and I went down like a ton of bricks shrieking like a banshee. "Mother trucker!" I cried out when my left knee landed hard on an abandoned Rubik's cube the moment Sam threw open the door and burst into the room.

"What's happening? Are you okay? Is anyone hurt?" Like the trained professional he was, he assessed the room for threats and visibly relaxed when he figured out what had happened.

"The only thing hurt is my ego." I sat up and rubbed the spot that had landed on the toy. "And my knee, but I think I'll live." Whether I recovered from the utter mortification of having him walk in on that particular display of grace and agility remained to be seen.

Sam grinned down at me and held out a hand to help me up. Keeping the grunting to a minimum, I grabbed hold and did my best to not stare at the way the muscles in his forearm flexed as he hauled me back to my feet. Hopefully, he'd believe I was flushed from the fall and not because of the butterflies his touch had awakened in me.

"Maybe I should reconsider the hike I planned for our evening," he quipped.

The corner of his mouth quirked up in a small smile that grew when I blanched at his comment. A hike? He hadn't said anything about a hike! I glanced down at my shoes and at the darkness outside the window.

"Uh, if we are going hiking, I'm going to need better shoes and a quick change of outfit." I was dressed for a warm-ish restaurant, not a nighttime hike in the snow.

It wasn't until Sam laughed that I realized he'd been joking. He squeezed my hand and pulled me closer. "I would be very, very sad if you changed out of that incredible outfit," he whispered in my ear. Louder, he said, "I was kidding. There are much better ways for us to spend an evening than freezing our toes off in the dark."

"That's what she said!" Stacey's wisecrack only made my face hotter.

"We should get out of here before I manage to break a bone or someone says something even more embarrassing," I said. The potential for mortification was high if we stayed any longer. As the thought crossed my mind, Sam placed his hand on my lower back and my knees wobbled alarmingly enough that he grabbed my arm with his free hand.

"You okay? Are you sure you didn't hurt yourself more than you thought?" His concerned frown made the butterflies in my stomach riot, but I somehow managed to smile back at him.

"I'm fine. Really." To demonstrate how not hurt I was, I stomped my feet on my way to the coat hooks by the door and winced when my knee twinged. "Okay, maybe not one hundred percent fine, but well enough to go wherever you had in mind."

Relief made his eyes shine. "That's fantastic news. I promise there will be no strenuous activity of any sort."

We both made a concerted effort to ignore Stacey's boo of protest and made our way to the door after I slipped on my parka.

With my hand on the doorknob, I turned around and addressed the crew on the couch. "Make good choices. Be kind. And please don't stay up too late."

Stacey grinned impishly. "Was that intended for just Aurie or all of us?"

"I'll let you be the judge of that," I said with a smirk and pulled the door closed behind me with a resounding click. "Let's get out of here before they think of a reason to call me back in."

Sam needed no further encouragement. He tugged my hand, and we raced down the stairs, and my knee barely hurt at all as I flew after him.

THIRTEEN

It was an absolute lie. My knee throbbed as I hobbled after Sam to a small red pick-up that had seen better days.

"Hang on, the passenger door sticks a little." He grimaced as he jiggled the handle and heaved the door open with a grunt. "It's not fancy, but it is clean!"

"It's perfect." I smiled and took the hand he offered to help me get into the higher-than-expected truck cab. The interior of the pick-up was roomier than anticipated and my stomach did a weird little flip-flop when my eyes landed on a bench seat where I'd expected to see bucket seats. I was still debating where to sit when Sam hoisted himself into the driver's seat.

"So? Where are we going?" I asked, more to break the awkward silence than out of curiosity. He could have been taking me to the dump for all I cared. I was dressed up, out of the house, and alone with a man who made my insides feel funny, what more could I possibly want? My body shivered in response to the question, and Sam glanced over at me with a concerned frown.

"Are you cold? Sorry. I should have left the truck running. It's freezing out here. But don't worry, it warms up fast. And, uh, you can sit closer to me if you want. For warmth!" He hurried to add, his face turning a delightful shade of pink.

"Sure, I bet that's what you say to all your dates," I teased.

"That's not…" He let his voice trail away, blushing even harder, and turned the key in the ignition. The truck came to life with a roar and warm air blasted out of the vents.

"Oh, that's nice," I said, rubbing my hands together in the stream of hot air. In my hurry to leave the house, I hadn't taken the time to pull my gloves out of my jacket pocket and my hands were tingly from the cold. Sam put the truck into drive and pulled out into the street. "You still haven't told me where we're going."

"It's a surprise," he said with a cheeky grin. "I think you're going to like it."

"As long as we're not hiking in the snow, I'm sure I'm going to love it."

It took a few blocks for my hands to warm up and for both of us to relax into the easy banter we usually enjoyed.

Before long, Sam was regaling me with a story about a visit he'd been forced to make to a woman's house earlier in the week because her neighbors had called in a noise complaint.

"She couldn't understand why they didn't think the baby goat she was keeping in her apartment was as cute as she did," he laughed. "We had to explain to her that it was against city ordinances to keep livestock indoors and help her find a nearby farm that would take the goat in. The neighbors were quite grateful. Apparently, the poor thing had a lot to say and said it loudly, all day long, and it had once eaten a bouquet of flowers that had been left on their doormat."

"It sounds like they weren't fans," I said, giggling.

"Yeah, no." Sam glanced at me and smiled. "Are you any warmer?"

"Yes. Thanks. It's toasty in here."

"Good, because we have…" he paused and turned the truck off the road, "arrived!"

I'd been so caught up in his story I hadn't noticed that we'd left Portney behind and had arrived close to the coast. Deep darkness surrounded the truck, and if it hadn't been for crashing wave sounds, I would have had no idea Sam had parked on a bluff overlooking what I could only assume was the ocean. The truck's headlights only illuminated the prickly bush right in front of us. Everything beyond was pitch black and when Sam cut the lights, the black only grew more intense.

"Okay, that's way darker than I expected," Sam said wrestling his phone out of his pocket. He turned the flashlight on low before tucking the device into a little compartment in the center console. "Better?" he asked, glancing over at me.

I nodded, grateful for the gentle glow. I wasn't a huge fan of the dark most days. Out here, on a deserted bluff...a cold tingle ran down my back and made the hairs on my arms stand to attention. I was in a car, in the middle of nowhere, in the pitch black with a man I didn't know all that well, and no one knew where I was. Every single warning my mother had ever uttered popped into my head, but I shushed them and forced my thoughts into another direction.

Cassie, you are being ridiculous. You aren't a fifteen-year-old hitchhiking on her own in the middle of the night. You're a grown-ass woman in a car with a guy you've known for months. He's a cop, not a mass murderer!

As quickly as the fear appeared, it vanished. I was with Sam for crying out loud. The guy I called when I was in danger. He was the opposite of dangerous and scary. To further reassure myself, I stole a glance at him, and my breath caught in my throat.

He was just so damn handsome. Not in the way Max had been classically good-looking, but in the angle of his jaw, and the squareness of his chin, and oh, the color of his eyes.

Whoops. He was looking right at me, and I was staring like a lovestruck teenager. My chuckle came out forced and uncomfortable. The easy banter we'd established during the drive had gone out at the same time as the lights and I had no idea how to get past the awkward silence building between us. "Ugh, why is this so weird?"

"Oh, I'm so glad it's not just me." Sam laughed, throwing back his head and some of the tension in the truck dissipated. "I know what will help. Hold please." He held up a finger and twisted around to rummage in the small space behind the bench seat. It took him a moment, but he crowed a triumphant 'Aha!' and tossed a woven plaid blanket onto the seat between us before pulling out a cooler he dropped on the floor between our feet. The second time he turned around to rummage behind the seats, he brought out a thermos and two travel mugs. "Tah da!"

"If that's hot coffee, be warned, I might ask you to marry me," I teased.

"You might want to wait and see what's in the cooler before you propose," he replied, waggling his eyebrows suggestively. He grinned as he balanced the thermos on the dash so he could pull a wide armrest out of the seat-back and settle it between us. "See? I can do magic, too." His blue eyes twinkled in the soft glow of the phone's light, and the butterflies in my belly sprang into action.

His eyes met mine and held on, inviting me to wade into their depths. The kindness and laughter dancing deep in them reminded me why I had agreed to go on this date in the first place. Sam was warm, friendly, and held nothing back. He was an open book who delighted in being read, the polar opposite of Max whose blue eyes were icy cold and closed off. For years I'd tried to see past the surface and had gotten nowhere. I leaned into the warm inviting pools of Sam's eyes. As if drawn to me, Sam also leaned forward, but just as our foreheads were about to touch, I jerked away. Surprise flared in his eyes, but with an awkward chuckle, he gestured at the thermos like I hadn't ruined a potential moment. "Coffee? It's not going to be Crystal quality, but I brew a pretty decent cup."

My head spun as I stammered out a yes without looking his way. Another second and our lips would have been touching. His looked so soft and inviting, and he smelled so damn good. Why hadn't I leaned in? What had possessed me to jerk away?

Sam was saying something about the coffee beans he'd brewed, but I was so focused on his lips, I couldn't hear what he was saying. What if he hadn't been closing in for a kiss? What if I'd imagined the whole thing? I mean, why on earth would he want to kiss *me*? Who could possibly want to kiss a 40-year-old single mom who had clearly let herself go in recent years? Max always acted like the thought of kissing me made him a little sick to his stomach. I was an idiot for assuming that Sam would want to put his lips on mine even as I couldn't seem to stop thinking about my lips on his.

I bet his lips would be soft. Soft and firm. He looked like a good kisser.

Hot shame washed over me, and I looked out into the darkness. I was too old for these games. Too old to be sitting in a cold car second-guessing myself and my date. Too old to be regretting a kiss that probably hadn't been about to happen.

I clutched the mug Sam handed me and buried my face in the steam, hoping he wouldn't notice my flushed face. What if he thought *I'd* been throwing myself at *him* and had changed my mind at the last second? That was almost more mortifying. What had I been thinking?

You weren't. You were diving into those warm pools and letting yourself go for the first time in... well... forever.

And that right there was the problem, wasn't it? I couldn't let myself go. I had a kid, a dad, a bakery, and people who relied on me. I didn't have time to lose myself in someone's eyes, or in a romantic relationship. I had responsibilities, dammit.

My heart fluttered, but I couldn't tell if it was in response to realizing how frustrating it would be to be pulled between wanting to be with Sam and the never-ending demands of my life, or in protest at what I was about to do.

"I'm sorry," I said, as he was opening his mouth to speak. "Oh, sorry about that too. Go ahead."

He chuckled awkwardly. "I was going to say the same thing. I'm sorry if I did something to spook you." He put his mug down on the armrest between us and looked deep into my eyes. "Cassie, I really, really want to kiss you. You have no idea how much I want to. How long I've wanted to."

The butterflies in my belly sped up, but I ignored them. "But..."

Sam took a deep breath and glanced out into the darkness. Out of the corner of my eye, I saw a muscle in his jaw tick. "But it wouldn't be fair to you."

Huh? I tilted my head to the side and frowned. "Come again?" That was the last thing I'd expected to hear him say.

"It's a bit cliché, I know, but I just got out of a relationship. It's complicated." He looked at me again. A tiny smile quirking up the side of his mouth made his dimple pop, and it took every ounce of self-restraint I had to not reach out to caress his cheek.

"Well," I said, both because it was true and because I was desperate to bring a real smile back to his face, "funny coincidence, but I was about to say the exact same thing."

His eyes widened, but he didn't seem all that surprised. "Max?"

"You know it." I shrugged halfheartedly, ignoring my violently protesting butterflies. "Yeah. It's messed up. I've been divorced for over six months. And it's not like Max and I were... uh... how do I put this delicately... tangoing on a regular basis before then."

He grinned at my euphemism. "Very delicately put. I like it."

I grinned back and continued, "but it still feels too soon." I shrugged a shoulder, "I like you, Sam. I like being with you. You are kind and considerate and you make me laugh. Being with you feels like a vacation from my life. And oh, do I need a vacation from it sometimes. But I'm damaged goods, and I just know I'd find a way to mess this up. Which would be devastating because then I wouldn't have you in my life at all."

"That would be sad. I am pretty spectacular," he teased. His smile softened and he reached across the armrest to cup my face in his hand. "Cassie, I really like you too, and I like being with you. I'm okay with waiting until we're both ready if you are. I have a feeling it'll be worth it."

He pulled my face toward his and rested his forehead against mine. He smelled woodsy and comforting and I nearly wept at the feel of my head in his hand. I could have stayed there forever, but he lifted his face and placed a gentle kiss on my forehead that shattered my resolve. In the most uncharacteristic move I've ever made, I grabbed his face in both my hands and pulled his lips to mine.

For a fraction of a second he resisted and I started to panic, but his lips relaxed, and, with a low groan, he cupped the back of my head and pulled me closer.

I closed my eyes and sank into the moment, blocking out everything other than the feel of his lips against mine, the woodsy smell of his skin, the slight prickle of his beard stubble rubbing against my upper lip, and the feel of his strong hands holding me so gently. By the time he parted my lips with his tongue, I could no longer make out the hysterical voices in my head. The future didn't matter. The past didn't matter. There was only Sam and me, our lips together, and the feelings swelling inside me.

Our kiss could have lasted ten years, and it still would have been too short. I couldn't remember the last time I'd lost myself so deeply in a moment. More importantly, I didn't want to try. My heart cried out when Sam's lips left mine, and he put his forehead back against mine with a sad little sigh.

"So worth it," he murmured, and I chuckled.

The moment the world around us came back into focus, the clouds parted letting through the light of the full moon and revealing the ocean spread out in front of us.

I looked over at Sam and placed my hand on his cheek in a perfect echo of his earlier gesture. "That was..." I shook my head and sighed, "amazing. But I'm sorry I did that to you. Because I'm more sure than ever that this," I gestured between us, "can't happen right now. There's only so much of me to go around and if we tried, I'd want it all to go to you, and I just don't have that luxury."

He pressed his cheek into my hand and smiled sadly. "I'm not sorry you kissed me. It only confirmed what I knew. We are going to be amazing together one day. Not today. But one day. Mark my words. In the meantime, I'm glad I get to have you in my life, however that looks." He reached forward and placed a gentle kiss on my lips. "Now, are you hungry? Because these lobster rolls aren't going to eat themselves."

I gasped and clasped my hands together. "You remembered!"

Sam laughed. "How could I not? You raved about lobster rolls all summer."

"But... but the shack is closed for the winter!" I'd nearly cried the day they'd put up a closed sign.

"I know a guy who knows a guy," Sam replied with a tiny shrug. Despite his nonchalant attitude, he was doing a terrible job of hiding the proud delight in his eyes.

He handed me a lobster roll and grinned at the look on my face as I unwrapped it. Despite the intoxicating scent of butter, lemon, and toasted bread teasing my senses, my heart stayed heavy and bruised and my soul was still protesting my decision.

You can't, Cass. You have Aurie and Dad and the bakery and mounds and mounds of work to fill your days. Not to forget the fact that there's an insane old witch out to get you. What are you going to do? Give her more ammunition to use against you? Don't be ridiculous and selfish. You already got your wish. You get to live the life of your dreams. Isn't that enough?

As my teeth sank into the buttery lobster, it was hard to ignore the tiny voice howling 'no!' in the back of my head.

I smothered it with another bite. It was going to have to be enough. I had too many people counting on me to give in to selfish impulses.

FOURTEEN

W hen I woke up the next morning, my eyes were crusty like I'd cried in my sleep and grief sat heavy on my chest. It didn't take a rocket scientist to figure out why.

You're making the right choice, Cassie. Yes, he's gorgeous and you could get off on his scent alone, but you're a grown-up and grown-ups have to make sacrifices for the good of their families. Shake it off, buck up, and let's get this day started already.

As mean as it was, my inner voice wasn't wrong. If I didn't have the bandwidth to take on a relationship, I certainly didn't have enough to mope about it.

I managed to hold it together through the painfully slow morning. At some point after Sam had dropped me off, the snow started falling with a vengeance and it was still coming down hard. Christina had headed home as soon as she put the last batch of bread in the oven and the Brewhahas had texted one after another to beg off. I couldn't find it in me to blame any of them. I was half tempted to crawl back into bed myself. Only the most adventurous of our regulars braved the blizzard to get their caffeine and carb fix, leaving me endless amounts of time to catalog all the ways my life was going off the rails. At the very least, I could be thankful there was no sign of another impending destructive catastrophe. In my already pitiful state, I didn't think I could face another epic disaster.

"I'm sorry I was such a pill yesterday. I was way out of line, but are you seriously telling me you don't think any of the stuff going on around here can be attributed to Margie? Not the bizarro hex bag hidden in the kitchen, the faucet exploding, or the entire dairy order going sour in record time?" My eyes almost bugged out as Crystal shook her head.

She shrugged. "I'm sorry, it doesn't strike me as her style." When I quirked an eyebrow up, she amended her statement. "Okay, maybe the hex bag. Though, honestly, it was a little amateurish for someone with her power. I'm sure if she wanted to curse you, she could have done a much better job without leaving something so obvious behind."

I hesitated as her words sank in. It was true that she was the most powerful witch in town and that the bag had been crudely made. "But still," I said, not willing to let it go. "You don't think it's weird? All that stuff happening at the same time?"

Crystal made a dubious face and tilted her head from side to side. "Fine, I'll admit it's a little too much at once to be coincidental. But I don't think you have enough to go on to pin it all on Margie. I still think she'd come at you in a much sneakier, underhanded, devastating way."

Our conversation was interrupted by a snow-covered customer bursting in to get out of the storm, but Crystal's words kept spinning in my head. It was true that Margie preferred a long game rather than a slap-in-the-face approach to dealing with her foes. But if she wasn't responsible for my string of bad luck, it left only one question, who was? And how was Margie connected? I might be willing to accept she didn't have a direct hand in everything that had happened, but she was definitely involved somehow.

When the customer bundled himself up and darted back out into the snowstorm, Crystal wisely opted to focus on tidying her coffee bar supplies instead of picking up where we'd left off. I ruminated as I reorganized the take-a-book-leave-a-book shelf and inventoried the mugs I liked to keep on hand for customers who fell in love with the ones we used in the bakery.

"Hey, before I forget to tell you again, I need some more pumpkin butter. I'm almost out," Crystal called out from behind the counter.

"Tim is dropping off my produce order tomorrow. I'll see if he has any more pie pumpkins." I looked down at the two books in my hands and grumbled. "Haven't I already shelved these?" I shook my head. "I'm sorry, I'm a mess today. And the snow is only getting worse. We should call it a day, don't you think?"

Crystal glanced out the window and made a face. "You're probably right. I doubt anyone else is going to venture out in that mess."

It didn't take us long to cover the unsold pastries and loaves of bread and move them into the walk-in pantry. Much to my relief, after stepping in to rescue me from myself the day before, Christina had also come in at her usual time to make today's bread. While things hadn't been as warm and comfortable as usual, she hadn't mentioned our altercation, and I wasn't dumb enough to bring it up first. If Christina left me for good, I might as well call it quits on the whole deal.

"So, is there something else going on, beyond thinking that you've been hexed?" Crystal asked, side-eyeing me as she slammed the fridge closed. "How did your date go last night?"

I had to give her props for waiting a whole hour before asking. "Ugh. It's a whole thing. I need sustenance to tell you all about it." I glanced at the clock and tilted my head. "Want to come upstairs? I haven't told Stacey anything yet. If you make the coffee, I'll grab a few pastries."

"It's not like I had plans," Crystal said with a laugh. "And I'm dying to know why you're not on cloud nine this morning."

"Coffee will make me spill all, I promise."

"Then I'll be right up with the goods!"

As predicted, Stacey was giving the Mr. Coffee machine the evil eye when I entered the kitchen holding a plate piled high with the pastries that wouldn't keep.

"Is the easiest coffee machine in the world giving you grief?" I joked, sliding the plate onto the table. The baleful look Stacey shot me in reply was so pitiful I took mercy on her and let her know Crystal was coming up with lattes.

"Oh, thank you," Stacey said, dropping into a chair and picking up a cream cheese and apple Danish. "It's not that I can't get that thing to work, it's that it never gives me the kind of coffee I actually want to drink."

I chuckled. "That would be because it's a simple drip coffee machine and you only drink super sweet coffee drinks designed for teens with amped up metabolisms."

"Exactly my point." She dropped her head on her arm and yawned. "Sorry I didn't make it down for coffee this morning. I stayed up way too late working after we tucked Aurie in bed, and I overslept."

"You didn't miss anything. The blizzard kept everyone away. In fact, it's why I'm up here now. It's a mess out there. We had a few die-hard coffee addicts come by this morning, but I doubt anyone else is braving the storm for a pastry or two."

"That bad?" Stacey hauled herself out of her seat and pulled open the shades. "Oh, wow. It's really coming down! Guess it's a good thing Shane is with her dad until I get home from Bali." In a surprising turn of events, Dylan had refused to let Stacey take Shane out of his life for good and followed them north. For the first time, Shane was seeing her father on a regular basis and loving every minute of it even if Stacey was skeptical about his renewed passion for parenting. He would undoubtedly vanish soon, but for the time being, we were both glad Shane was getting the attention she deserved.

"Who's ready for a cup of real coffee?" Crystal called out as she stepped out of the stairwell and into the kitchen, holding up a tray loaded with five steaming mugs.

"Five? There are only three of us here," I said, frowning.

She shrugged and put the tray down. "Figured Aurie would be up soon, so I made her a cup of hot cocoa."

"And you called my dad down," I finished for her, eyeing the plain black coffee sitting next to a stack of sugar packets.

"Come on, you know I'm not the only one dying to hear about your big date." Crystal grinned.

"Oh, yeah!" Stacey perked up and reached for a large latte mug. "Mmmm. I want to hear every sordid detail." She glanced past me down the hall and whispered, "preferably before the rugrat joins us."

"There are no sordid details," I said, sighing. "It didn't go the way you're all hoping it did."

"So, no kiss?" Stacey lowered her mug and looked at me over the rim. There was no stopping the blush that flooded my face. "Oh! Ho ho! So, there was a kiss!"

The door to the outside landing crashed open a moment before she finished crowing.

"You let that boy kiss you on a first date?" my father barked before turning to wrestle the door closed. "It is nasty out there."

"Dad, he is hardly a boy and I'm not a teenager you need to police. I'll kiss whoever and whenever I want."

"Can I kiss anyone I want, too?" Aurie asked, stumbling into the kitchen with Willow at her heels. She rubbed her face and peered at us through sleepy eyes. "What are you all doing up here anyway? Did something else explode in the bakery?" Her eyes flew open, and she glanced at the stairs with a worried frown.

"Sorry we woke you, bug. Nothing to worry about. No disasters of any kind... well, other than natural ones. There's a crazy blizzard out there so we closed early. Crystal made you hot cocoa if you want!"

"Yum!" she said, sliding into the last available chair. "Thank you, Crystal," she added hastily when I frowned at her. "You didn't answer my question, Mom. Can I kiss anyone I want whenever I want?"

The twinkle in her eye made it clear she was teasing me, so I stuck my tongue out in reply.

"I don't know, Cassie," my dad said, shaking his head at our antics. "You might not be mature enough to make that call on your own."

"Touché," I said, tipping my mug at him and narrowing my eyes at him as he opened a third packet of sugar. He stuck his tongue out at me when he caught the look on my face. Aurie giggled and I found it hard to stifle a grin. My heart was going to hurt for a while, but moments like these were ultimately why I'd told Sam we couldn't be together. I'd missed so many years with my dad, I didn't want to miss out on more by adding something else to my already overloaded plate.

When I described how the date had gone and explained my reasoning to everyone around the table, they all looked at me with varying degrees of horror and disbelief.

"Wait, wait. Let me get this straight." Stacey held up her hands. "You told a good-looking, attentive, kind man who somehow found you lobster rolls in the dead of winter that you couldn't date him because…" she paused and squinted, "you wanted to have breakfast with your dad and your daughter?" She sat back and shook her head. "I am so confused right now."

"It's more than just that!" I protested.

"It doesn't sound like it," Crystal said. "I'm confused too. You were so excited about the date!"

"I was! And it was great! But we *both*," I stressed the word and glared at all of them, "decided we had too much going on to get into a serious relationship right now."

"So, make it a casual thing." My dad shrugged and slurped his coffee. "No one's telling you to marry the guy."

"I don't get it," Aurie said with a frown. "I thought you liked Deputy Sam."

I bit back a frustrated groan. "I do. He's a great guy. And we're still going to be friends. Nothing is going to change. I promise, kitten."

"Hold up!" Stacey held up a finger. "If you cockblocked him..." my gasp interrupted her, and she looked around like she'd forgotten who was in the room. Thankfully, Aurie had either not heard or not understood what she said, because she didn't look up from trying to catch mini marshmallows on her spoon. I glared at Stacey, and she continued in a more subdued tone. "Uh... if you... let him down gently..." The snark in her voice made me roll my eyes. "At what point was there kissing?"

At that, everyone looked up at me, even Aurie whose eyes were as round as saucers. My face heated to an uncomfortable degree, but I'd promised details and that was the only vaguely interesting one to share.

"After we decided not to date," I muttered.

"You said no, and he kissed you?" My father's adorable indignation only made me blush harder.

"Ah, no. I ah, I'm the one who kissed him." Amidst Crystal and Stacey's hoots and hollers, I hurried to clarify. "I just needed to know what I'd be missing out on." When their hoots only got louder; I snapped my mouth closed and dropped my head in my hands.

"And...." Stacey leered at me.

"It was magical," I muttered.

"Knew it!" She grinned like she'd won a prize.

"And then we agreed to not get romantically involved," I reminded them all.

"Mom? Am I supposed to not date anyone so I have time to spend with you and Grandad?" Aurie asked, looking up from her hot chocolate.

"Uh, no. You're not supposed to date anyone because you're twelve and you're too young." Where was this coming from? Was she old enough to be developing crushes?

"Duh." She rolled her eyes and gestured with her spoon. "Later, when I'm like thirteen, then should I not because of you and Grandad?"

"Later, when you're fifteen… or sixteen," I corrected when my father frowned, "you can date whomever you want whenever you want. Well, not on a school night. And… well, we can figure out reasonable parameters when the time comes, but no, you shouldn't *not* date because of it would take time away from us."

She frowned and peered at me through her lashes. "So how come you and Deputy Sam aren't going to date because of us?"

I swallowed another frustrated groan. "It's different for me."

"Why?" Her frown deepened.

"Because it is. Grown-up lives are complicated. There are other factors at play. Do you have any homework for tomorrow?" I asked in a feeble attempt at changing the subject.

"No homework. Miss Amy said we're going to spend the day preparing for our field trip." She bounced out of her seat and ran to the window. Cupping her hands against the glass, she peered out into the storm and turned back, her forehead creased in worry. "Do you think they're going to cancel our field trip?"

"They better not," my father grumbled under his breath. "Most exciting thing I've had to look forward to in weeks. And that's saying something."

"Nah." Crystal dismissed her concern with a wave. "The blizzard will be over by then and the roads will all be cleared. Nothing to worry about. I doubt they even cancel school tomorrow."

My heart lurched in my chest. The snow was falling so hard I couldn't see out the window. "Are you serious?" I asked Crystal. "That doesn't seem... safe."

"Eh, Mass kids. Hardy bunch. Plus, the roads will all be plowed by the morning. You'll see. By Tuesday it'll be like it never happened. This is a nothing storm. Just you wait until winter really gets going!"

I shivered at the thought and not for the first time wondered if settling in Massachusetts was a wise move for
someone who'd never had to own a snow shovel.

"If you say so." I shook my head and glanced out the
window again. It was unclear how that mess would be
gone by morning, but if Crystal said it would be, I was
willing to take her word for it. I shrugged and pinned
Aurie with my best no-nonsense-mom-stare. "In that case,
Stinkerbelle, you better go clean up your room so you can
find your gloves, hat, *and* scarf," I admonished.

"Do I have to?" she whined, shoving her mug away from
her.

"On the double, please."

With another loud protest, Aurie pushed away from
the table and skulked away to her room. The odds of her
looking for her winter gear, let alone finding it, were slim,
but at least I wouldn't have to answer any more challenging
questions.

"Want to know what I think?" Stacey asked the moment
Aurie's door slammed shut.

"No," I grumbled, draining my mug.

Her eyes danced with mischief. "I think that Max really
did a number on you and now you're scared of getting
hurt. And you're making up excuses because that's easier
than facing what's got your panties in a twist."

"My panties aren't in a twist," I protested. "And I'm not scared." Three dubious faces stared back at me. "I'm not! I'm just busy! With the bakery, and Aurie, and... you know... everything else!" I didn't need to see their bemused expressions to know my protest lacked oomph. "And anyway, Sam also said he was also getting over a relationship! It's not just me!"

Crystal scrunched up her nose and tilted her head to the side. "He did? I mean... Arguably, he and Kristy were a serious item, but they broke up well over a year ago."

Kristy? I winced at the pinprick of jealousy the name evoked. He wasn't mine. Because I wanted it that way. What was the point of being jealous? If he wanted to be with this Kristy person, I had no right to stop them. Not even if it made my heart ache to think of him cupping another woman's head in his hand and pressing his warm lips to hers.

Oblivious to my inner turmoil, Crystal continued. "They broke up because she got a big shot job in California, and he realized he wanted to live here more than he wanted to be with her. I honestly don't think he was even all that torn up about it."

"Then why bring her up at all?" I frowned, replaying the conversation in my head.

Could he have said that to give me an out because he noticed my hesitation? Suddenly, my arguments for avoiding a relationship didn't seem so reasonable anymore. My heart plummeted into my stomach. Had I passed up on something incredible because of fear? Because of Max? A flicker of the rage that had consumed me for months flamed to life. Was Max ever going to stop ruining all the good things in my life?

No matter how hard I tried, I couldn't ignore the little voice in my head that piped up to correct me. Was *I* ever going to stop letting Max ruin all the good things in my life?

"What did I do?" I curled forward and dropped my face in my hands. Their sympathetic expressions were harder to bear than their earlier dubiousness.

"Honey, take it from a man who has lived a life steeped in regret," my father said, his eyes filled with unfathomable sadness. "The heartache you might experience from risking too much is far easier to bear than the heartache you get from missing out on something amazing."

The truth in his words took my breath away for more reasons than one. It was too late for my father to go back and take the risk he'd avoided. I could only hope it wasn't too late for me.

FIFTEEN

As Crystal had predicted, the storm raged through the afternoon and stopped in the early evening, leaving behind a magical winter wonderland. The plows worked through the night and the morning dawned to functional roads and a bustling town. The only hint that we'd been besieged by snow the day before were the towering mounds of dirty snow piled up in various parking spots along the sides of the street.

"It's like nothing happened. Like there was no blizzard or anything out of the ordinary yesterday," I marveled to Crystal, not for the first time that morning. She humored me with a grin.

"Do we need to go outside and have a snowball fight?" she teased, then groaned when she saw my eyes light up.

"Can we?" I gave in to the child-like bubble of excitement threatening to burst in my chest and clapped my hands together. "Oh!" I flapped my hands. "Let's pelt the other Brewhahas when they arrive!"

It wasn't my fault that I was so excited. Getting Aurie ready for school and listening to all the fun she was going to have with her classmates in the snow at recess had given me intense FOMO. We had miraculously found a left and right glove, and I told her that wearing a mismatched set was her punishment for not taking better care of her belongings. To be fair, the faintly guilty look on Willow's face was making me wonder if maybe Aurie wasn't the culprit behind all the missing winter gear.

My excitement must have been contagious because Crystal yanked off her apron with a mischievous chortle and hurried to slip into her parka.

"Hurry! Juliette just walked out of her store," I hissed, pulling on my gloves.

"You know she can't hear you, right?" Crystal replied, peering through the glass door. "Crap. Hattie's on her way too!"

With no time to spare, slipped through the bakery entrance and started shaping as many snowballs as we could hold. Never one to let anything go unnoticed, Hattie whooped the instant she saw us come outside and started gathering her own snowballs. Juliette, looking a little preoccupied, never saw the first volley come her way.

"Whuh... what... whuh?" she sputtered, wiping snow off her face. "What is happening?"

Instead of answering, we pelted her with another round, then, without missing a beat, Crystal turned and started lobbing snowballs in Hattie's direction. It took Juliette another few beats to catch on and a few more beyond that to get into the spirit of the game, but Amy dove right in when she got out of her car and saw what was going on. After that, all bets were off. My hastily stockpiled stash of snowballs ran out in seconds, and I found myself fending off attacks while using my air magic to gather snow into something vaguely resembling more balls. It would have been easier if I hadn't been laughing so hard I could barely catch my breath.

Hearing the telltale whizz of a snowball heading my way, I spun around to counter and started to lose my balance. The tightly packed ball of snow Hattie had thrown right at me hit the air shield I hastily threw up. I was in the middle of a victory dance when my foot lost traction and slipped out from under me. With a dull thud, I fell back into a snowbank and stayed there, doing what I could to catch my breath between bursts of giggles. I could not remember the last time I'd had this much impromptu fun.

"Time! Time!" I called, waving my arms and legs in the air feeling a whole lot like a turtle stuck on her back.

"Oh! Snow angels! Good idea!" Crystal replied, throwing herself into the snow next to me. She'd barely started swishing her arms back and forth in the snow before Hattie lay down in the snow on my other side. With a laugh, I stopped trying to get up and joined them in their exuberant attempt to create snow art.

"You too, book fiend," Hattie proclaimed, grabbing Juliette by the arm and yanking her down next to us. My cousin sputtered in protest then gave in long enough to create the smallest snow angel imaginable.

"I don't remember making snow angels being this wet," Crystal gasped between bursts of laughter.

"And that is why you don't do them without snowpants," Amy quipped, looking down at us and smirking. How she's avoided being pulled down was beyond me.

"Or this cold!" Hattie added.

"Well, this is my first, so I have nothing to compare it to, but I'm pretty sure my underwear is never going to dry," I said, finally hauling myself to my feet and beating the snow from my backside. "Hot chocolate anyone? I think we've earned it."

Hattie and Crystal scrambled to their feet and hurried inside with Amy while I pulled Juliette back to standing and helped her brush the worst of the snow off her back.

"You okay? We kind of ambushed you, there."

"Kind of?" She quirked an eyebrow and smiled, but I sensed an undercurrent of annoyance under her amused façade.

"I'm sorry! We thought it would be fun! Well, I thought it would be fun. I never got to do this as a kid." I made a face and the smile I got in return was a lot warmer.

"It's okay! And it was fun! I just... I have a lot on my mind. I'm sorry I'm being a party pooper."

"Nonsense." I tucked my arm into hers and pulled her toward the bakery. "It's not like you're supposed to enjoy being pelted with frozen water and thrown onto ice." I winked at her and smiled when she chuckled in reply. "So, what's going on with you? What's on your mind."

Her smile faded and she wrapped her arms around herself. "It's nothing. Really. Did you make any of your persimmon goat cheese twists this morning? I've really been craving one."

I stopped at the door and looked at her. "You don't have to tell me what's bothering you if you don't want to, but you know I'm here for you if you need me, right?"

"I know." She squeezed my arm and gave me a sad smile. "I know, but I promise it's nothing. Really."

It would have been easier to believe her if she'd looked me in the eye when she said it, but if she didn't want to go into it, I wasn't about to push it.

While Crystal prepared some of her enchanted hot cocoa, Juliette used her elemental water magic to pull the moisture from all of our clothing and deposit it in Crystal's little coffee station sink. Within minutes, we were all warm and dry in minutes, which meant everyone had plenty of time to jump all over me about my botched date with Sam.

Stacey came down the stairs with her overnight bag slung over her shoulder just in time to add her two cents to the conversation. Not surprisingly, everyone was on the same page. All of a sudden, the reality of what I had passed up came crashing back down, smothering the lightness and joy that had blossomed during our romp in the snow.

"I know! I'm the world's biggest idiot, and you're all appalled I turned him down! Can we please let it go?" I said, throwing my hands in the air and storming off to grab a bin for the dirty dishes.

"Is that really what you heard us say?" Hattie asked, a concerned frown on her face.

"Well, it's what you all said. Multiple times," I snapped, dropping mugs and plates helter-skelter into the bin.

"That's not what we said at all!" Crystal protested.

"Not even close," Amy added.

"Whatever. I get it. I botched it. Can we all move on, please?" My voice cracked, and I glanced away so they wouldn't see the tears gathering in my eyes.

"Aw, babe!" Stacey got up and tugged the full bin out of my hands so she could pull me into her arms. "We do not think you're an idiot or that you botched anything. We are worried you are once again going to put your needs last and prioritized everything and everyone else in your life."

"Kissing a man is hardly a need," I joked, swiping at the tear that had escaped.

"Yes, it is!" Hattie, Stacey, and Crystal replied as one while Juliette squirmed uncomfortably in her seat.

"See? Juliette agrees with me! I can happily live without a man in my life."

Her head snapped up, and she shook it emphatically. "I did not say that, and I do *not* agree."

"You don't say?" Crystal replied, raising both her eyebrows and propping her chin on her hands as she focused on Juliette. "Please, tell us more."

The cold had already turned Juliette's cheeks pink. Crystal's attention turned them an intense shade of fuchsia. "There's nothing to tell, I agree with all of you. Cassie shouldn't prioritize everyone else over her physical needs." My cheeks flushed hot enough to match hers, but she didn't meet my supportive gaze. She stood abruptly and looked around for her purse. "I have to get out of here. I have a... a delivery arriving any minute."

With a quick 'bye' she was out the door and hurrying up the street, her hands shoved deep in her pockets and her face pulled down into her jacket.

"Was that weird?" Stacey asked, watching her through the window.

"Eh." Hattie shrugged. "That was Juliette. Sometimes she's a little weird. We all still love her." She got to her feet and looked around for her coat. "That said. I have to jet, too. The bunnies made a real mess last night. I think the storm freaked them out."

Stacey said a quick round of goodbyes, promising to check in from the beach and to think warm thoughts for us all, and darted out to her car when the first customer of the day arrived, cheeks reddened from the cold and a wide smile on her face. "Brrr! It's nippy out there! Good day for hot cocoa."

Crystal chuckled in reply and made her way to her drinks station. "One hot cocoa, extra whip coming right up!"

"Oh, I really shouldn't," the customer protested, but she relented when Crystal raised an eyebrow in reply. "Oh, sure, why not! I'm sure I deserve it for some reason or another."

There was still a Sam-shaped weight on my chest and the constant nagging worry caused by the unsolved hex bag mystery lurked in the back of my head, but goofing around in the snow with my friends had lightened my heart enough that I found myself humming as I finished tidying up. Maybe things weren't quite as dire as I'd imagined.

SIXTEEN

The way people swarmed the bakery, you would have thought the storm had lasted for weeks rather than less than a day. It was a good thing we had the pastries that hadn't sold the day before or we would have run out of food hours before closing.

When the tornado of customers finally waned, I quickly checked the time. "Hey, Tim should be here any minute with my produce order. Are you going to be okay up here by yourself? If not, I can send Christina out, she's probably close to done in the kitchen."

Crystal was shaking her head 'no' when the door opened with a cheery jangle, and a large group walked in, slapping their hands together to warm them up. She nodded sheepishly. "Yes, please."

My timing was near perfect. The instant I sent Christina to Crystal's aid, Tim, the produce guy, knocked on the back door, grinning and waving at me through the glass.

Produce day wasn't as fun in the dead of winter as it was in the spring, but it was still the highlight of my week. Tim and I had a deal, he threw in a few surprise items with my standing order, and I rewarded him with the resulting experiments. He'd raved for weeks about the caramelized grilled persimmon hand pies I'd made him once. This week, I was surprising him with peppermint bark brownie bites I'd whipped up using the extract made from his hothouse mint. I was looking forward to watching him lose his mind over them.

"Did you bring me anything good today?" I asked, rubbing my hands together in anticipation and stepping out of the way so he could push the dolly stacked high with produce crates through the door.

"Like I ever bring you anything bad," he replied with a laugh. The dolly thumped when he stood it upright, and I grinned like a little kid on their birthday.

One by one, he checked the crates off on his clipboard after hoisting them onto the counter and gestured with a flourish after depositing the last one. "Your produce, kind baker, as requested."

"My humble thanks to you, kind sir," I replied with a mock curtsy. "I can't wait to see what you've brought me."

"I think you're going to be very happy." He grinned as I wrestled the top off the crate closest to me.

The first indication that something was wrong was a faint buzzing sound that got louder when I lifted the lid. The second was the swarm of massive black flies that erupted from the crate the instant it was open.

"Ew! Ew! Ew!" I screamed, jumping back and waving my hands frantically in front of me. Bile rose in my throat every time my hands connected with the flies. "Oh! I'm going to vomit. Tim! What the hell?"

"I...what? I don't understand!" Tim swatted at the flies with a look of abject horror on his face. "I packed that crate myself less than a half hour ago. There wasn't a single bug. There aren't bugs anywhere in my warehouse." He looked affronted at the mere thought.

"Well, they're here now!" I batted away the flies hanging out on the paper covering the produce and groaned when I lifted it up. The apples might have been pristine when Tim loaded them into his truck, but all I saw was a pile of bruised and moldy fruit.

"Cassie, I swear that's not what they looked like when I picked them out for you this morning. You know I would never!" His voice rang with truth as his panicked eyes flicked back and forth from the mangled fruit back to me.

"What's going on?" Crystal demanded, poking her head through the swinging doors. "All that screaming is starting to worry customers." When she saw the flies covering every surface of the kitchen, she turned green and gagged. "What the what?" She tore her gaze from the horror show and glared at Tim.

"It's not his fault," I said. As my eyes darted around the room in an effort to assess how far the flies had spread out, something about the baseboard near the back entrance caught my attention. Before I could figure out what, a swarm of flies flew right at me. "Ugh. So nasty," I grumbled, swatting them away.

"How can it not be his fault? He brought the damn produce, didn't he?" Her gaze shifted back to the blanket of flies and the corner of her mouth twitched with revulsion. "Can't you? You know...?" Jerking her eyebrow suggestively, she pursed her lips together and blew.

Tim was too busy cracking open the other six crates to see if anything else was spoiled to notice her gesture, and I shot her an annoyed look and shook my head before returning my attention to the wall that had caught my eye. I didn't think he knew anything about magic, and this was hardly the moment to induct him to the club.

"Everything else is fine, Cassie," Tim said with a relieved look on his face. "I am so sorry. I have no idea how that happened. But I can run back to the farm and get you some fresh apples."

"That is a phenomenal idea," Crystal hurried to say. "But there's no rush. Tomorrow is fine. Right, Cassie?" I tore my eyes away from the baseboard next to the door and saw she was glaring at me, waiting for me to chime in.

"Oh, yes. Thank you, Tim. Tomorrow's fine. I wasn't going to use the apples today in any case."

Blustering more apologies, Tim hurried out the back door and made his way through the backyard to the truck he'd parked on the street behind the bakery. It wasn't the easiest way to access the building, but he liked that it meant he didn't have to walk through the shop to get to the kitchen.

As soon as I closed the door behind him, I took a closer look at the baseboard. It was a tiny bit askew, like something had made it move. Maybe the water had made it shift when the kitchen had been flooded.

"What is up with you?" Crystal snapped the moment he was out of sight. "Why aren't you freaking out?"

"Oh, I am, trust me," I said, throwing open the door and calling on my wind magic to sweep every last fly out the door. I slammed the door shut and spun around, glaring at her. "I am so done with this bull. Who does she think she is? That stunt could have gotten us shut down for days if not weeks." I clenched my fists to keep my hands from shaking and took a tremulous breath.

"Who are you talking about?" Crystal frowned, looking utterly confused.

"Who do you think?" I yelled. When she flinched, it made me want to scream. I growled under my breath and dropped to my knees next to the wonky baseboard.

"Cassie, Margie isn't out to get you! Stuff happens!" Crystal replied sounding beyond exasperated with me.

"Oh, yeah? Then how do you explain this?" I turned to her, gesturing to another, larger hex bag. This one was filled with more bones and a wider assortment of flowers and sticks than the last one, all of it coated in a viscous oily substance that looked all sorts of wrong. It had fallen out the moment I'd touched the baseboard. Not even well hidden.

"Cassie!" Crystal cried, as I leaned forward to get a better look at the little bag. "Don't touch it!"

"I know!" I rolled my eyes at her. "Hand me the tongs, will you?"

Her eyes were wide with fear when she handed me the tongs, and she hopped out of my way as I walked past her to drop the bag in the sink.

"Can you please agree now that everything that has been happening isn't coincidental?" I didn't know what I would do if she still didn't believe me.

Crystal took the tongs out of my hand and poked at the little bundle making a dubious face. "I'll grant you that it's weird, but you still have no proof that it's Margie."

"Ugh!" I groaned, fighting back a scream. "I do not understand why you can't just accept that there's something really hinky going on around here!"

Crystal rolled her eyes and sighed. "Look, I'm sorry you're so upset, but I still think you're overreacting." She looked over my shoulder and gestured to the pastry torch we'd used to burn the first hex bag. "Hand me that, would you?"

Biting my lip hard, I did as she asked and watched her brandish the torch at arm's length and point it at the hex bag in the sink. The fire made the salt crystals clinging to the little pouch spark as it licked up the sides and engulfed the whole thing.

I was mesmerized by the way the fire was lapping at the contents of the bag when the pouch exploded. Green flames shot out in every direction before extinguishing themselves as quickly as they had flared.

"Whoa!" Crystal screamed, jumping back. She blinked rapidly and shook her head. "What was that? What's going on, Cassie?"

I frowned at her confusion. "What are you talking about?"

She looked at me with wide eyes and jabbed a finger at the burning charm. "That? What is that?"

"Have you completely lost your mind?" I asked, narrowing my gaze at her. "Are you pranking me right now?"

"No! I genuinely have no idea what the heck is going on!" She looked both horrified and scared and I found I didn't like the combination at all.

"It's... it's..." I gestured to the wall where I'd found it. "It's a hex bag! I found it in the wall. Two seconds ago. You were right here!"

Crystal frowned and shook her head. "I would remember that."

"If you weren't here, why are you holding the blow torch?" I asked, throwing my hands in the air.

Crystal looked at the torch in her hand and back at the sink, her frown deepening. "Fair question." She took a step closer to the sink and peered down at the smoldering charm. "Cassie, I have no idea what that thing is." Her voice quivered enough to let me know she was really freaked out.

I tilted my head and frowned. "Hold up. Do you remember the other one?"

Her head snapped up and she looked at me. "There was another one?" she whisper-shrieked, glancing at the swinging doors that were thankfully staying shut despite the noise we were making.

"Yes!" It was my turn to sound exasperated. "You were right here when we found it! Remember? It was right after the milk spoiled?"

Crystal paled and her eyes widened. "Wait. I think I remember. But it's super fuzzy like it's behind a gauzy curtain. What on earth is happening to me?"

I frowned again and held up a finger before going to the swinging doors. There was no one at the counter, but Christina still looked wild-eyed and frantic. She hurried over when she saw me peering at her through the crack in the doors.

"What is going on, Cassie?" she hissed.

I gestured her over and whispered, "do you remember when the faucet exploded?"

She made a face and shook her head as if to clear it. "Huh, that's weird. I remember it happening, but the memory is foggy. The faucet exploded. Your dad and Hattie went to turn off the water. And that's about it. Why?"

"What about when the whole dairy order went bad overnight and stank up the place?"

Her eyes widened and she shook her head slowly. "It's all so fuzzy."

"Last question, do you remember the hex bag we found under the island?"

She grimaced and stared at me, shaking her head, then her eyes widened further. "Oh, wait... I think I do! We had to move the island to remove it. How could I forget that? What is going on?"

All the customers appeared to be happily enjoying their coffee and pastries, so I motioned for her to come into the kitchen where Crystal was poking at the burnt charm with a concerned frown on her face.

"Right, so, I'm obviously no expert, but I think that thing," I pointed at the sink, "was designed to make you all forget about the weirdness going on around here." The relief at having found it was almost disproportionately overwhelming. For the first time in days, I didn't feel the prickle of annoyance and frustration that had kept me on edge. "I think it may have also been messing with my emotions."

"What? There's more?" Crystal's eyes looked like they were going to bug out of her head.

"Well, yeah... there's the whole dairy order gone bad deal." I frowned. "How do you not remember that?"

Christina blanched and Crystal's hand flew to her mouth and her eyes grew as wide as I'd ever seen them.

"Oh! I do remember!" Her face fell and she turned to me. "Cassie, I'm so sorry we didn't believe you!"

"I was so rude to you!" Christina whispered. "I am so sorry!"

"You weren't nearly as rude as I was." Thinking about how I'd spoken to them made my face hot with shame.

The tears I'd successfully fought back earlier came back with a vengeance. I'd been so annoyed about everything that had happened, I hadn't realized how much it was bothering me that no one was taking my concerns seriously.

"Wait, so how do we all feel now about how I want to blame Margie for all this?" I asked, bracing myself for more ridicule.

"Oh, for sure. No doubt in the world that crazy witch is behind all this. I can't think of anyone in this town who has that kind of mojo." Crystal pursed her lips and shook her head. "No doubt about it."

"But she's never been alone in here. There's no way she could have planted anything without one of us knowing," Christina protested.

Dread washed over me. "Can I leave you two in charge? There's something I have to do, and I don't think it can wait until we close."

SEVENTEEN

The icy wind slapped me in the face, but the anger bubbling deep inside kept me warm as I stormed down the street to find Margie, clutching the least moldy of the apples in my gloved hand. The utter conviction that Margie hadn't acted alone and that I knew exactly who she had manipulated into doing her dirty business made my gut roil.

It made me sick to think that my refusal to rise to her ongoing provocation had pushed her to enlist Juliette's help. It made me even sicker to imagine what she must have done to strong-arm my cousin into acting against me.

Unless Juliette participated of her own volition.

I banished the thought with an angry shake of my head. She would never. I knew without a doubt that I meant as much to Juliette as she did to me. We had both grown up lonely wishing we had a close family member our age. Finding each other this late in life had been the greatest surprise of an eventful year. I doubted she would jeopardize our relationship lightly.

Margie had been trying to goad me into a confrontation for weeks. She wanted it to be loud and public so that her smear campaign could finally take root, but I had consistently refused to rise to the insults she threw or the rumors she started. The only logical explanation was that she'd upped her game out of desperation.

In my defense, I had no desire to get into a fight of any sort with her. She was stronger, older, and had way more experience wielding magic than I would ever accrue. Plus, our feud existed solely in her head. I had better things to do than get into a pissing match with someone who would undoubtedly win.

A wet-sounding squelch made me realize I'd accidentally tightened my fist around the rotten apple, and I swallowed convulsively until the urge to throw up had passed. It was unclear why I'd needed to bring proof of her treachery with me, but I'd grabbed the spoiled fruit on a whim and neither Crystal nor Christina had stopped me. I was somewhat regretting my hasty action.

There was no telling where Margie was lurking, but before I confronted her, I needed to talk to Juliette to get to the bottom of her involvement.

Despite my inner turmoil, the cheery display windows of *The Book Nook* made me smile. Juliette always did a stunning job of decorating her tiny store window. This week, in anticipation of the upcoming romantic holiday, she'd displayed an assortment of romance novels and included a sign that read "Take the hint, fellas." Her dry wit didn't often come out to play, but when it did, it rarely disappointed.

The smile died on my lips, and my stomach leapt into my throat when I caught a glimpse of Juliette and Margie facing off over the store counter. From my perspective, it looked like Margie was tearing into Juliette, and my cousin was letting her browbeat her without saying a word.

The most infuriating thing was that I knew exactly why she was letting her do it.

The one and only time I'd stood up to Margie she'd almost killed my daughter, and I had been forced to acknowledge how powerful she was compared to me. With the DA in her pocket and almost a decade of magical experience under her belt, doing my best to de-escalate conflict was the best way to keep my family safe.

There was little doubt that Juliette was an old hand at playing the same game.

In the name of protecting everyone I loved, I had resigned myself to putting up with her countless little attacks. My customers were loyal, and my cooking spoke for itself. But putting my livelihood at risk? Possibly bringing the health department down on me? That was almost as bad as directly hurting my family. And here she was doing that right in front of me.

The only thing my cousin wanted was to be allowed to run her quaint little bookstore in peace. Her ideal day involved hunting down the perfect book for her customers and offering a welcoming, comfortable haven to anyone seeking a moment of respite from their lives. She was sweet, gentle, and kind, and the last thing she deserved was to be manipulated by a woman whose last ounce of decency had long since flamed out.

Especially if the intent of her manipulation was to destroy our relationship.

I hesitated for a moment, watching the two of them argue through the window, but when Margie reached over the counter and grabbed Juliette's cardigan, I snapped and stormed into the bookstore, brandishing my disgusting piece of fruit.

"It's your own damn fault, you know. If you weren't at-tached at the hip with that...that...little..." Margie sput-tered, but before she could spit out the word I knew was about to come out, I slammed the door shut behind me and they both jumped.

Juliette only looked relieved at the interruption until she saw the look on my face. When her eyes dropped to the nasty apple clutched in my hand, her lips pulled back in disgust.

Frustration and fear would have overwhelmed me if anger hadn't gotten there first. It was all I could do to wres-tle the primal scream building in my chest down enough to attempt saying something coherent.

"You! You!" I stormed toward Margie, waving my hand around hard enough that little flecks of apple flew in every direction. I flinched when a particularly large chunk land-ed on a stack of books on a display table at the front of the store. Juliette had once explained to me the process of sending back unsold books and it hadn't sounded like fun. "You evil, vindictive, horrible old witch, congratulations, you finally found the line!"

Margie straightened up and a humorless grin bloomed on her face. "Oh?" She raised her eyebrows and looked down her nose at me. "And what line would that be?"

"The 'you pissed me off far enough to get me to react' line," I growled. Instead of the surprise I was hoping to see appear on Juliette's face, all I saw out of the corner of my eye was guilt and the feeble control I had on my rage snapped. "You tried to destroy my bakery. You ruined my dairy order and now you've tainted my produce shipment! I know you want me gone, but you know what you did instead?" I took another step closer until we were almost standing nose to nose. I rose up on my toes and screamed down into her face. "You pissed me off. And you know what that did? It made me more determined than ever to stay right here and to make sure you're the one who leaves. You might think you're safe from the law, but I don't give a rat's ass. I will run you out of town, and I'll do everything in my power to make sure you can never come back here again. You messed with me and my family one time too many, you old hag." As good as it felt to say, it wasn't half as satisfying as seeing Margie cringe away from the moldy apple I was shaking in her face.

She stepped back until she bumped up against the best-seller table and schooled her expression until she once again looked haughty and a little bored with my theatrics.

She shook her head and smirked. "I'm sure I don't have the faintest idea what you're going on about."

I wanted nothing more than to grab her by her obnoxiously bright parka and shake the smug expression off her face, but as I was about to launch myself at her, she glanced at Juliette, and her self-satisfied smile grew.

Getting kicked in the chest would have hurt less than having my suspicions about Juliette's involvement confirmed.

"I'm so sorry, Cassie," Juliette whispered hoarsely. "I didn't want to. Please believe me."

"Oh, shut your whiney sniveling mouth," Margie growled at her granddaughter. "You know I didn't make you do anything you didn't secretly want to do." She smirked at me and I knew without a doubt that ruining our relationship had been the end goal all along, destroying my livelihood was just icing on that particular cake.

"Cassie, that's not true. You know it's not true! She... she..." she covered her face with her hands.

Her despair only fueled my rage. "All you do is lie and manipulate people, Margie. You're two-faced and both of your faces are evil and corrupt. How does it feel to know everyone hates you and they're only nice to you because they're scared, or because they pity you?"

"You little... how dare you speak to me like that," Margie hissed. "You're nothing. No, you're less than nothing. You're a speck of dirt on my shoe, and you know what I do to things too disgusting to deal with? I obliterate them."

With a flick of her fingers. Margie sent a wave of energy in my direction, and I braced myself for what was coming. She was adept at controlling all the elements, so anything was possible, but I wasn't all that surprised to see a flicker of flame land on the mangled apple in my open hand.

Flames engulfed the rotten fruit, and with a shriek, I tossed the fireball away from me and watched in open-mouthed horror as it shot toward a stack of free community newspapers. I frantically flapped my hands, calling on my air magic to shift its trajectory, but instead of having the desired effect, the fire absorbed the air and tripled in size and intensity.

"No!" I howled. "Juliette, where's your fire extinguisher? Wait! Hold on, maybe I can remove the air and starve the fire."

Juliette shot me a dubious look and glanced at the stack of papers the fire was rapidly devouring. I narrowed my eyes and focused all my attention on the flames and the air around them. For a moment, it seemed like my plan might work. The flames started shrinking and hope surged in my heart. Then, for no reason at all, the flames redoubled in intensity. An evil cackle pulled my attention from the burning stack of papers.

"What are you doing?" I cried, rounding on her. "Are you *trying* to burn Juliette's shop down?" Smoke was rapidly spreading through the store and panic made my heart shudder. Even if we got the fire extinguished, the damage we'd caused was already significant.

"Maybe I am. Maybe it'll teach the little brat a lesson on loyalty." With a manic grin, she flung both hands forward and poured even more energy onto the hungry flames.

All color leached from Juliette's already pale face making her dark eyes look bigger than ever.

I tried one last time to pull the air from the fire, but with a careless gesture, Margie snatched control of the element from me and directed the stream to the dancing flames.

"I'm sorry, Juliette. She's too strong for me," I cried, letting my useless hands drop to my sides.

The fire leaped for the stack of flyers on the counter and curled itself around the small wooden rack Juliette used to display book-themed stickers and started lapping away. She roused herself with a shake of her head when the fire reached the other side of the display case.

"The fire extinguisher! It's in the kitchen!"

I glanced from the spreading fire to the door leading to her tiny chicken-themed kitchen. She was on the right side of the counter, but did she have time to make it out safely? It only took one glance around the store to unglue her feet and propel her to the kitchenette, her shoulders tight with determination.

A tendril of fire reached for her as she moved away from the counter, and she threw a dirty look at Margie who smirked back at her.

The woman was not in her right mind. That much was obvious. But did she really mean Juliette harm? I couldn't tell. Her manic grin only grew as Juliette didn't reappear right away.

The moment Juliette vanished into the kitchen, the fire started working its way toward her cash register. If the store was going to go up in flames, the least I could do was grab what money she had on hand.

Darting past the larger flames, I pounded on the register until it released the cash box. I hissed from the heat of the metal when I grabbed it with my bare hands and glared at Margie one more time for good measure. She cackled back at me and, with a final satisfied look around the store, turned and walked out into the street like fire wasn't swirling around her feet.

The fire nipped at mine as I sped after her, but by the time I pulled the door open to toss the cash box outside, she was nowhere to be seen.

"Hurry up, Juliette! It's spreading!" The shrill note of my voice must have made her step it up because she burst through the door clutching the fat black and white polka-dotted ceramic chicken from the tiny kitchen table under one arm and brandishing a fire extinguisher in her other hand.

"What the hell, Cassie! This is more than just spreading!" Her outburst left her gasping for breath. The smoke made it hard to see, but the fire had spread far beyond the counter into the store itself where it was devouring the books, leaping from one shelf to the next with apparent delight.

Juliette and I both came to the conclusion at the same time that there was no way her small kitchen fire extinguisher would slow it down, let alone stop it. I yanked my shirt over my mouth and watched helplessly as she pointed the fire extinguisher at the fire lapping at her feet and cleared herself a small path to the store's front door where I was waiting for her muttering 'hurry, hurry, hurry,' to myself under my breath.

Speaking up, I called to her, "Hurry! Hurry! Hurry!" She glanced over her shoulder at the fire lapping at her heels and sped up.

"Oh, no! The money from the cash register!" she gasped, looking frantically back at the counter.

"I tossed the cash box outside," I reassured her. "As long as your grandmother didn't nab it on her way out, it should be safe." Grabbing her arm, I tugged her outside and into the middle of the street. With an angry whoosh, the fire exploded behind us and my breath caught in my throat. One more second and we wouldn't have made it out unharmed.

Juliette spun around and let out an anguished cry. Lunging toward the burning building she cried out, "But the.."

"Let it go. It's gone." I pulled her into her arms and held on tight as she struggled until the fight went out of her, and she collapsed against me in a heap of sobs. Tears streamed down my face as I watched everything she loved go up in flames. Deep inside me, my anger burned hotter than ever. I didn't know how I was going to do it, but I was going to make Margie pay dearly for this and for everything else she'd done.

EIGHTEEN

"I'm so sorry, Juliette," I murmured, glancing over at my cousin. She hadn't taken her eyes off the burning building since the first responders had arrived. Thankfully, they'd managed to douse the worst of the flames before the buildings on either side caught on fire. Neighbors milled around, looking at times horrified and titillated by the unfolding drama. Juliette hadn't acknowledged any of their concerned glances, leaving me to wave and give everyone a thumbs up in response to their questioning expressions.

Unlike the butterflies in my stomach, she also hadn't reacted when Sam pulled us out of the way of the firemen. He sat us on a stack of blankets he'd placed out of the wind under the overhang of the store across the street. She didn't acknowledge that he wrapped a large blanket around our shoulders or that he said he'd be back in a few minutes to check on us.

The longer she sat there, eyes fixed on the burning building, face wiped clean of any emotion, the worse I felt. My heart was still racing from the terror of not seeing her come out of the little kitchen, and I was having trouble breathing, though I had a feeling that had more to do with guilt and fear than smoke inhalation. Meanwhile, the only sign she was experiencing any feelings was the white-knuckle grip she had on the ceramic chicken clutched in her hands. Even with my mental guard wide open, I couldn't get a hint of what she was feeling. Though that could have been because, much to my relief, over the last few weeks my friends had gotten better at instinctively blocking me from tasting their emotions.

How was it possible that a crate of rotten fruit had devolved into a disaster of this magnitude? If I hadn't risen to Margie's bait, we wouldn't be here right now. I'd be working happily in the bakery and Juliette would be snug and safe in her store, surrounded by her beloved books. A sob lodged itself in my throat, making it even harder to breathe.

Margie's latest attack hadn't been any worse than previous ones, so why had it triggered me so hard? I'd wanted to protect my family, and in the process, had destroyed everything my cousin could call hers. I reached for Juliette's hand and squeezed, hating how it lay limp and cold in mine.

"Maybe if I'd been practicing my magic more..." I let my voice trail away knowing full well it wouldn't have made a difference and wouldn't have been possible. Between the Brews & Hues fair, the dozens of Thanksgiving pie orders, and the endless stack of Christmas cookie orders that had poured in before everyone had fully digested their turkeys, I had barely had a moment to catch my breath let alone work on my craft. Somehow, I didn't think using magic to make pots fly into the sink was the kind of practice that would have made me strong enough to combat Margie's fire magic.

Juliette didn't react for so long, I was sure she hadn't heard me speak, but after a long silence, she replied without taking her eyes off her burning shop.

"She's not just the matriarch because she's the oldest witch in town. It's also because she's the most powerful. Practicing all day every day wouldn't have made you strong enough to stop her. I've been practicing magic my whole life and I couldn't stop her. But I deserve this, Cassie. This is just punishment for everything I've done to you in the last month." Juliette's tone was eerily flat. She could have been commenting on the fact that the wind had briefly died down rather than talking about how her grandmother had destroyed her store as she stood in it.

"What? What are you talking about?" I pulled back so I could get a better look at her face, but she was still staring into the flames. "Juliette, that's absurd. You didn't deserve this. No one deserves to lose everything they own." My mouth snapped shut. She couldn't mean it. It had to be the shock talking.

"You don't know what I've done," she replied, tensing up as I slipped my hand into the crook of her arm and leaned my head against her shoulder for a moment.

With a sigh, I lifted my head and stared at the ground between my feet. "Let me guess. Your grandmother held something or other over you and strongarmed you into placing a few hex bags in my kitchen?" She didn't react so I continued, "maybe she made you do a few other things I haven't yet discovered? And, what, we had a bit of a plumbing catastrophe and some milk and produce got spoiled. None of it caused any permanent damage. No one got hurt. This," I gestured to the inferno blazing in front of us, "is not fair punishment for anything."

"She wanted me to do way worse," her voice was so low I had to lean closer to hear what she was saying. "But I couldn't bring myself to do it, not even when she threatened to hurt Aurie again. I'm so sorry, Cassie. I was doing what I could to protect you all. I figured that if I placed the hex bags and deployed her enchantments, I could manipulate them enough to make them, I dunno, less potent, less dangerous." She hugged the chicken to her chest and rocked over it. "I'm so sorry. I'll understand if you never want to speak to me ever again."

In response, I hugged her arm tighter. "She threatened Aurie?"

Juliette nodded, "she said the potion Aurie drank in the fall was nothing compared to what she had in mind. And she threatened Willow. She was just so determined. I didn't know what else to do."

Any anger I'd harbored toward Juliette for enacting her grandmother's evil plans, or for at least not standing up to her demands, evaporated. Gratitude strong enough to silence me for a moment settled in its place.

After a few beats, I found my words. "Thank you. Thank you for risking your grandmother's wrath for Aurie. Thank you for doing what you could to keep us safe. I... I don't know how I'll ever repay you." I waved helplessly at the fire. "Especially not now."

"It's enough to know you don't hate me." She squeezed my arm and leaned against me. "This feels like a nightmare. I'm going to wake up any minute and I'll be in my bed, in my apartment, surrounded by my things, and everything is going to be how it should be."

The magnitude of her loss hit me like a punch to the gut, and I gasped for air. I did the only thing I could and wrapped my arm around her shoulder and pulled her close to me.

"I've got you. You know that? You're not going to go through this alone." My voice cracked, and I tried to swallow the lump in my throat.

She gave my arm an absentminded squeeze and murmured "I know," in an unconvincing tone. We sat there, holding each other, until an EMT came to lead her away to his truck to tend to her injuries.

My chest got tighter as she walked away without looking back. It had taken Juliette months to relax into our relationship and to open up to me. She sometimes tensed up for no reason, but for the most part, she'd been at ease around Aurie, my father, and me. I couldn't bear to think about how all of this might close her off from us again.

"You okay?" Sam asked, after walking over and squatting in front of me. He peered at me with concern. "Are you hurt? Did you get burned?" He looked me over for obvious signs of injury and when he didn't see any, he ran his hands down my arms and gently took hold of my hands. His touch made my whole body tremble, and the warmth of his hands in mine crashing against my sorrow for Juliette made me dizzy.

"Whoa. Let's get you bundled up again." I let Sam pull my blanket back around my shoulders and shook my head a few times to clear it. When I opened my eyes to look at him, the concern on his face had only deepened. "Cass, you didn't answer. Are you hurt? Is there something I'm not seeing?"

The smile I attempted came out a little crooked, so I tried again with slightly better results. "I'm okay. I promise. Just shaken, I think."

A wry smile softened the concern in his eyes. "Well, that's understandable."

"And my heart aches for Juliette." I glanced over at my cousin, sitting in the back of an open ambulance, letting the EMT wipe soot off her emotionless face as she stared at the burnt-out shell of her home over his shoulder.

"That's understandable, too." He looked over at her and shook his head. "I can't fathom what she's feeling right now." He swiveled his head back in my direction. "Or you, really. Do you think you're ready to tell me what happened?"

Tears welled up in my eyes, and I blinked them away before they could fall. "It all just happened so fast. One minute I was holding a piece of rotten fruit and the next everything around us was on fire." A shudder shook the blanket loose and Sam tugged it back over my shoulders.

"Wait, what? What does rotten fruit have to do with anything." He was trying so hard to be gentle and sweet, but he couldn't stop his cop voice from peeking out.

"Ugh," I groaned. "You better sit down."

He settled himself next to me and scootched as close as possible. I told myself I was leaning into him because he was warm and not at all because I couldn't resist touching him, but there was no denying how my heart fluttered when he wrapped his arm around my shoulders and pulled me closer.

"Right, so, rotten fruit?" he prompted.

Guilt flared deep in my gut and for a moment, my throat swelled shut. Rubbing it helped a bit, as did Sam murmuring that I could take all the time I needed.

Guilt, shame, horror, and the kind of sadness that seeps into your bones and makes you wonder if you'll ever be happy again writhed together in a ball of angst that made it hard to breathe, let alone speak. But as much as I wanted to pretend it had all been a terrible, terrible accident, there was no hiding from my role in the disaster. As I watched the firemen put out the last of the flames, I walked Sam through what had happened, not leaving out a single detail, not even the way the explosion of flies had al-

most made me throw up. His calm, comforting de-
meanor changed when I got to the part where Margie had
encouraged the flames instead of helping me quell them.

"You're sure about this?" I frowned at him, annoyed
that he'd think I'd lie about something so serious, and
he smiled. "You know I'm only asking so I have it on
the record that Margie intentionally set fire to Juliette's
store."

"Oh." I paused to replay the incident in my head. "I'm
not sure I'd say her intention was to set fire to the store.
I think, at first, she just wanted to startle me. But then
the newspapers caught on fire, and it was like it triggered
something deep inside her. It's hard to explain, but I saw
in her eyes the moment she decided to keep me from
putting out the fire. Then, when Juliette went to get the
fire extinguisher, the fire went crazy. I could be wrong,
but I got the distinct impression she was egging it on."

The wind had picked up again, and Sam pulled me to
my feet, making sure the blanket was snug against my
shoulders. "We have to get the two of you inside before
you both freeze to death. I'm going to walk you to the
bakery and then I'll put out an APB on her."

A quick look in Juliette's direction showed me that
the EMT was just about done bandaging up the few
burns she'd gotten on her arms when she'd fought her

way through the store. "Nah, it's okay. We can walk there ourselves. It's not far."

He grinned at my pathetic attempt at a joke before pursing his lips and nodding. "Okay, if you're sure. Stay there, please, until I call you later. I don't think Margie will be hard to track down, but she seems to have flown so far off the handle, who knows what she might try before we catch her." His words sent a chill down my back, and I shivered inside my blanket cocoon. Misunderstanding the reason for my shudder, he rubbed my arms briskly. "Drink something nice and hot as soon as you get there, okay? Doctor's orders."

"Oh, are you a doctor as well as the deputy sheriff? I had no idea," I teased, happy to change the subject.

He tipped his hat at me and winked. He leaned close enough to me that his breath caressed my cheek when he spoke. "Oh, Cassie, there's so much you don't know about me." My face burst into flames when he turned and strode away, leaving me blushing and gaping at his retreating back.

NINETEEN

Juliette flinched as I approached. Until that moment, she'd been stoic, but the kind looking EMT must have been cleaning out a tender spot because she sucked in a short breath through her teeth. She didn't glance my way when I came to a stop next to her, but she didn't shrug off the hand I rested on her shoulder.

"I'm sorry. There was a lot of debris in that one. I think it was the worst of it, though." The genuine compassion in the EMT's tone caught me off guard and pulled my attention away from Juliette's pained expression. Despite his boyish good looks, he wasn't as young as he'd looked from where I'd been sitting.

"It's okay. It doesn't really hurt. Just a little sensitive." Juliette's attempt at a smile fell short.

"It probably will later, I'm sorry to say. But I have an ointment that should help. My granny makes it."

Something about the way he said the word ointment made me tilt my head. "Your granny's a..." Catching myself, I let my sentence trail off. There was so much supernatural chaos in my life, I sometimes forgot that not everyone knew about magic and everything that came with it.

His sheepish grin was surprisingly endearing. "A witch, yeah. Kitchen witch with healing abilities. I come from a long line of them." He glanced at the ambulance behind Juliette and chuckled. "I know. I know. I'm a total cliché. The son couldn't heal with magic, so he became an EMT. It wasn't my goal and yet..." He caught her staring and let his voice trail away. "Sorry, I ramble sometimes. How are you feeling?"

She took a moment to assess before answering with a half-hearted shrug. "I'm not sure how I'm supposed to feel." An unreadable expression crossed her face as she looked over his shoulder at the smoldering building. "It doesn't seem real."

A weight settled on my chest, and I squeezed her shoulder. I had been in the bookshop with her, and I still couldn't believe what had just happened.

"Well, I can't speak to the emotional component of what you've gone through, but hopefully you're not in too much pain. Are you having any trouble breathing? Is your heart racing?" He pulled a small flashlight out of his shirt pocket and pointed it first up one of her nostrils and then the other. When he prompted her to, she took a tentative deep breath and let it out without coughing. "Okay. That answers that. In that case, I guess you're done here. Take all the time you need, but you're free to go when you're ready. If you do start having trouble breathing, or your chest starts to feel tight, please go to the emergency room immediately."

Juliette nodded in reply, without taking her eyes off the ruins of her bookstore. He followed her gaze and sighed. "I'm so sorry. I loved your store, you know."

Her eyes focused on his face and recognition flickered in her eyes. "You come to the Saturday morning children's hour with..." She paused, screwing up her face as she searched her memory. "Zoey with a 'y.'"

His eyes lit up and a delighted grin split his face. "My niece. My sister's kid. Her mom has a standing thing on Saturdays, so Zoey and I hang out." Some of the joy fell from his face. "She's going to be so sad."

Juliette tensed under my hand. The children's reading hour was one of the highlights of her week. She went to a lot of trouble to pick the perfect books. Every so often she asked me to make themed cookies to make the event extra special. Her shoulder didn't relax, but a hint of a smile appeared on her soot-covered face and there was a teasing note in her voice when she said, "there's always the library reading hour."

He pretended to be pained by her comment. "Now that's just mean. Are you trying to pay me back for hurting you earlier?" Miss Bitsy tried, but the library was in dire need of renovation, and the children's corner was more drab than cheerful.

Juliette's wan smile grew a little, and I was able to take a slightly deeper breath.

While they were both looking at the building, lost in their respective memories, I snuck a peek at his name tag. Half of his name was hidden by his uniform, so I didn't see his full name until he turned around to check her bandages one last time.

"I think you're all set. Take care of her, okay?" He said, looking over at me for the first time since I'd interrupted them. "Make sure one of you calls me if her breathing starts to sound labored."

Juliette scowled, probably because he was talking about her like she wasn't there. But I shot him a grateful smile. "Thank you for everything, Sean. We really appreciate it."

"Thank you," Juliette muttered, but she managed to give him a genuine smile.

He beamed like she'd offered him the moon and handed her a card. "Here's my number. Please don't hesitate to call if you need anything."

"There you are! I've been looking everywhere for you both! I was worried sick." A sob caught in Hattie's throat as she came to a stop in front of our little trio and pulled us into her arms. Sean stepped back and busied himself with tidying his supplies. She pulled back and peered at both of our faces, her eyes wide with barely suppressed panic. "The two of you are okay? Right?"

Feeling Juliette bristle at Hattie's well-meaning attack, I did what I could to pull her attention onto me. "We're fine. Sean over here says we are cleared to leave."

"Oh, good." Hattie took a small step back and wrung her hands. "You'll freeze to death if you stay out here any longer."

"I'm fine," Juliette said, hopping to her feet. The instant they touched the ground, her legs wobbled, and she would have hit the deck if Sean hadn't grabbed her.

"Whoa there, take it easy. You've had a serious shock and it is freezing out here. Give yourself a moment." Her face flushed red with mortification, but she didn't pull her arm out of his grasp. If anything, I could have sworn she leaned a little into him.

"Are you sure you're good to go? Maybe we should go to the hospital to have you checked out more thoroughly." Hattie asked, concerned. It was disturbing to see her look so unsettled. She was usually the rock of our group.

"I'm fine." Juliette snapped. When Hattie's face fell, she softened her tone. "Sean gave me the all-clear and I don't think I could handle being at the hospital right now. I just want to clean myself up and have a hot cup of tea."

Out of habit, she looked over at the bookstore as she spoke. Tears rose in my eyes at the despair contorting her face.

While I battled down a sob, Hattie's fix-it persona snapped into place. She couldn't bring back Juliette's home, but she could make tea.

"I recently bought the most delightful oolong tea set. I've been looking forward to showing it to you." She placed her hand under Juliette's free elbow to support her as she attempted to find her feet again. Once Juliette was standing, Hattie made sure her blanket was snug, wrapped her arm around her waist, and started to shepherd her toward the pet shop.

I followed in their wake, grateful that Hattie had taken charge. We had a spare room, but the afternoon had drained me, and all I wanted to do was shower off the soot and crawl onto my couch and pretend I hadn't made everything my cousin owned go up in flames.

I was desperate to step into the welcoming warmth of my shop, to be surrounded by the warm homey smells of coffee and fresh bread, and to know deep in my bones that I was home and safe, but at the same time, I dreaded crossing the threshold, knowing how painful it would be for Juliette to be reminded of what she'd lost.

It wasn't you, and you know it. I rolled my eyes at the voice inside my head. I might not have been the one to fan the flames, but if I hadn't stormed out to confront Margie... If I hadn't antagonized her... I shoved the thoughts out of my head. There was no changing what had happened. And if Juliette didn't want to blame me, then I owed it to her to forgive myself too.

Pulling my head up and ignoring the pinprick of doubt in my belly, I hurried to catch up to Hattie and Juliette so I could give them both one last hug before Hattie mother-henned Juliette into her store and, presumably, up the stairs to her apartment.

"Coffee as usual tomorrow?" Hattie asked over Juliette's head as I handed her the cash box I had rescued from the fire. Other than the ceramic chicken Juliette still clutched, it was the only thing that had survived the flames.

"Of course," I replied with a smile. "Take care of my cousin."

"Of course," Hattie said with a little twinkle in her eye.

Juliette caught my hand and squeezed it. "I really don't blame you, you know that, right?" The candor in her eyes should have settled my stomach, but it wasn't wholly effective. Still, I smiled as warmly as I could back.

"I know. I love you, you know that?" I squeezed her hand back.

Her answering smile was as unconvinced as I'm sure mine had been, but before I could say anything, Hattie was tugging her away, and I let the scent of warm pastries and hot coffee lure me to my bakery.

TWENTY

Even after three rounds of shampoo and two of conditioner, I could still smell smoke in my hair. It even overpowered the warm scent of cinnamon and ginger in my tea, but Aurie and my dad had assured me that they couldn't smell it, so it was possible that it was all in my imagination. Maybe I'd never shake the smell of Juliette's books going up in flames.

I shook my head to dispel the image the smell brought to mind and tried again to focus on the silly movie Aurie had chosen for us to watch. I'd lost track of the plot around the time the main character had been turned into a princess against her will, but I'd stayed tucked into the corner of the couch, under a heavy quilt with her because I couldn't bring myself to move.

The reality of what had happened hadn't hit home until I'd come upstairs and she'd thrown herself into my arms releasing a sob strong enough to shake her from head to toe. Holding her tight, I murmured over and over that I was okay, and Juliette was okay, but she hadn't let go for a while. When she had released me, she'd stayed close by all evening, like part of her wasn't sure I wasn't going to vanish for real if she let me out of her sight.

All afternoon, I'd been so focused on everything Juliette had lost that I hadn't taken the time to acknowledge how much worse things could have played out. It was nothing short of a miracle that we had both walked out of that inferno alive. Margie could so easily have trapped us inside, part of me wondered why she hadn't. I shuddered at the thought. Then again, she had claimed that putting Aurie in a coma had been an accident, so maybe she really wasn't capable of murder.

Or maybe killing the two of you today didn't fit into her grand plan.

I ignored the cynical voice inside my head and snuggled down into the blanket, pulling Aurie against my side, fully expecting her to wriggle out of my embrace. She hadn't willingly cuddled with me in months, claiming she was too old for couch snuggles, but she didn't even stiffen as I tucked her against me. Her head settled on my shoulder, and I let the scent of her apple blossom shampoo soothe me.

Today could have played out a million different ways, but it hadn't. Juliette's things had all burned, but we had walked away with minimal injuries. I hadn't been ripped from my family, and Juliette hadn't been swallowed up in flames. It had been a horrible, shocking event, but it was impossible to deny how much worse it could have ended.

As much as I wanted to hold on to my guilt over provoking the incident, it paled in comparison to the realization that Juliette was alive because I'd pulled her out of the fire.

Aurie wiggled in my arms, pulling me out of the downward spiral of my thoughts and back into our cozy living room. I hadn't been able to bring myself to light a fire in the fireplace, but it was warm enough with just the central heat. I had a glass of wine balanced on the armrest, a pizza was on the way, and while I'd been showering, Aurie and my father had prepared a brownie that was starting to fill the apartment with the heady aroma of molten chocolate. I breathed it in and let out a slow breath that took with it all the stress over the cursed charms, the incidents in the bakery and the horror of the afternoon. My soul settled and for a moment, I let myself bask in the feeling that all was right in my world.

Guilt tightened my throat until I swallowed it down. Juliette and I were alive. Everything else was immaterial.

And when Margie was finally in jail, there would be nothing holding us back from living our lives to the fullest.

My father, glancing away from the movie that he was watching with a mildly baffled expression on his face, met my gaze and smiled. His greeting earlier had been gruff, but I'd seen right through his bluster. He was just as relieved to have me home as Aurie.

He parted his lips, but the doorbell rang before he could say whatever had been on the tip of his tongue.

"Pizza!" Aurie shouted, jumping out of my arms and battling her way out from under the covers. Her flailing arm knocked my glass of wine over, instantly turning the rug next to the couch crimson. Willow woke up out of a dead sleep and added sharp excited yips to the chaos as she bounced around, adding a layer of difficulty to Aurie's mad dash to be the first to open the door.

"Wait!" I called, extricating myself from the couch. "Don't open the door until you ask who's there!"

"Mom!" Aurie whined. "It's obviously the delivery guy. I can smell the pizza from here."

"Hey, don't sass your mom like that," my father grumbled. "If she says ask before you open, you ask before you open."

She had her back to us, but I knew without a doubt that she rolled her eyes as she called 'who's there?' through the door.

"Pizza delivery!" The laughter in the young male voice came through clearly and I bit back a laugh of my own.

"Thank you for humoring me," I said. "There should be cash in my purse."

"I've got it," my father muttered, pulling out his wallet and handing Aurie a twenty as she pulled open the door.

"Dad, don't be silly! Save your money." I left the words 'you don't have a job' unspoken. He was pulling a small pension from his trucking company, but it was barely enough to cover his weekly grocery bill.

He scowled at me and shoved the bill into the delivery guy's hand. "Keep the change," he growled, daring me to say something with his eyes.

My mouth was half open with a protest when I decided to let it go. We could have a conversation about his spending habits in the morning after we stuffed our faces with pizza and brownies and slept off the worst day of my life. We had nothing but time stretching out in front of us.

TWENTY ONE

Dreams of being caught in various raging infernos tormented all night and I woke up feeling both drained and relieved it was finally time for me to get out of bed and away from my nightmares.

With the malevolent charms gone, the unpleasant tightness at the base of my neck that had been plaguing me every time I stepped into the bakery kitchen had vanished. The low-grade anxiety that had gnawed at my stomach for weeks was also missing, and for the first time in as long as I could remember, nothing dragged me down as I rushed through my morning tasks.

The Brewhahas tended to start trickling in around seven, so I had plenty of time to get everything baked and displayed, but that didn't stop me from bouncing from station to station like an untethered balloon.

Christina grinned at me from behind a mound of bread loaves. "I haven't seen you this chipper this early in a long time."

"I know! I feel great." Guilt prickled at my conscience, bringing me down a little. "I mean, I'm upset about what happened and I'm worried about Juliette, but it feels so good to be in here without all that dark energy swirling around."

The small frown that appeared on her face as she glanced around the kitchen made me wonder how it was possible that I had been the only one affected by Margie's magic. I shook off the unpleasant thought and smiled at her.

"Maybe I'm just glad to be alive."

She grinned. "Well, I'm glad you're alive too."

Thinking about Juliette took a lot of the pep out of my step. Everything I touched or looked at was a reminder that she wasn't waking up in her own bed or pouring tea into her favorite mug. It was impossible to fathom what it would feel like to lose everything—home, business, belongings—all at once. At least when Max had told me we were through, I'd had time to go through our house to collect the things that really mattered to me.

According to the few texts Hattie had sent me throughout the evening, Juliette was doing okay. Hattie had seemed a little surprised that she wasn't more devastated over what had happened. I was anxious to see how she was doing for myself.

Despite my promise to myself that I would let Juliette set the tone for the morning, I couldn't stop myself from rushing her the instant she and Hattie stepped into the bakery.

"I'm sorry, Juliette. I'm just so very sorry," I said, pulling her into a hug. She squeezed me back and pulled away.

She met my eyes and narrowed her gaze. "I know you feel guilty, but it really wasn't your fault," she said sounding surprisingly firm. "My grandmother started the fire and encouraged the flames. You weren't even the catalyst. You were just a convenient pawn."

Her eyes radiated genuine sincerity, but it wasn't until I probed her with my magic that I fully believed what she was saying.

"But..."

She squeezed my hands harder. "You did me a favor, Cassie. I was in shock yesterday, but last night it occurred to me that you freed me. Don't you see that? I no longer owe her anything."

"Yes, but..." I couldn't shake the mental image of all her burned belongings.

"Just things," she said with a tiny smile that grew when my eyes widened in surprise.

"How did you know what I was thinking?"

"You, my dearest cousin, have the absolute worst poker face in the world. I don't recommend it as a backup living." She slipped her hand into the crook of my arm. "Now tell me, did you perchance make some of your honey pear turnovers this morning? Because that sounds exactly like what I want for breakfast." I hesitated another second, and she hugged my arm. "Cassie, this isn't the first time in my life that I have lost everything I owned. It might not even be the last. I know how to get through this."

"But this time is different."

"How so? Because it was my grandmother's fault? Sorry to break it to you, but she's not the first family member to betray me." She slipped into a chair with a self-deprecating smile.

The magnitude of what she said hit me hard and it took me a moment to catch my breath. "No, this time it's different because you don't have to deal with any of this alone. You have me, and my dad, and all the Brewhahas." I gestured to Hattie as she sat and to Crystal who was putting a tray of steaming mugs on the table. "You may have lost all your belongings and your store." She winced and I softened my tone. "But you haven't lost your real family. You haven't lost the people who care about you.

Whatever you decide to do next, we are here to help and support you. You are not going through this alone."

The combined taste of disbelief and loneliness flooded my tastebuds, but when I opened my mouth to protest, tears beaded up in the corners of her eyes. She blinked them away and plastered a grin on her face. "Cassie, honey, I adore you and everything you're saying, but if you don't get me some breakfast, I might have to hurt you."

I swallowed my words and smiled back. It didn't matter if she didn't believe me, we'd show her one action at a time. Starting with breakfast.

"What am I, a monster? Of course I made those turn-overs. They're your favorite. I also made those tiny donuts you adore."

"Oh, be still my heart." She clutched at her chest and pretended to swoon, making us all laugh. "It's a good thing I have to buy a whole new wardrobe."

Out of the corner of my eye, I saw Hattie and Crystal hesitate before chuckling awkwardly, but I went along with the tone Juliette was trying to set.

"I have a bunch of stuff in my closet that should suit you."

Juliette laughed and quirked an eyebrow, looking me up and down.

I grimaced. "Okay, maybe not suit, but it should at least fit." Even though we were roughly the same size and build, my wardrobe leaned more in the jeans and flannel shirt direction while she favored boxy pinafore-type dresses and turtlenecks. Where she'd found her clothes was a mystery to me. I was pretty sure L.L. Bean had stopped carrying those dresses back in the 90s.

Hattie snorted and shook her head. "We can go shopping this afternoon if you want."

"Oh! I love shopping!" Crystal clapped her hands with glee. "And I cannot wait to get you some fresh new duds."

Juliette looked pained at the thought. I couldn't blame her. Crystal's tastes ran to bright colors and hip designs.

We all laughed again when she stammered out a polite 'we'll see.'

"I mean, I hate to be the one to say it, but those dresses weren't doing anything for you." Crystal was choosing a pastry from the platter in the center of the table, so she didn't see Juliette's eyes suddenly fill with tears.

"I love those dresses," she murmured, not looking up at any of us. "They make me think of my mom. For years after she died, I stopped at every thrift store I came across and looked for them. I haven't found one in years."

Again, the magnitude of what she'd lost stole my breath away. It wasn't just things; it was memories and mementos.

"I'm sorry, Juliette." Crystal reached across the table and placed her hand over Juliette's and gave it a quick squeeze. "I had no idea. I meant no disrespect. We can look online, maybe put out some feelers on social media. I bet we can find at least a couple at vintage stores."

Juliette smiled, but there was no warmth in it. She shrugged and looked away. "It's okay. You're right. Maybe it is time for me to get a fresh look."

With no warning of any kind, Persimmon, the portly orange cat that had come with the bakery jumped onto her lap with a look daring her to tell him to get down. Juliette was smart enough to hold her hands up in surrender as he turned around a few times and made himself comfortable. She would probably never admit it out loud, but she looked somewhat comforted by his weight and presence. A loud rumble filled the room, and it took me a moment to locate its source. Had I really never heard him purr before? By the looks on everyone's faces, I wasn't the only one.

Persimmon's interruption allowed us to focus on our food and for a few minutes, the only sounds that filled the shop were happy eating noises and the cat's purr.

"You all know I'm fine, right?" Juliette asked, breaking the silence. Hattie arched a skeptical eyebrow in her direction. "All right, I'm not fine. How could I be? But I will be. I've been through worse before."

"You know, just because you've experienced trauma doesn't mean trauma is acceptable," Hattie said, looking serious.

"I know. But it happened. It's done. What's the point of crying over it?" Juliette shrugged.

Hattie shook her head. "Crying has its purpose."

"Meh." Juliette looked unconvinced. "Maybe it's not just my wardrobe that needs refreshing. Maybe this is a sign that I should start over somewhere new, where no one has ever heard of my grandmother."

Words failed me and I stared at her with my mouth hanging open. She couldn't be serious. I had waited my whole life to have family of my own and she was talking about leaving as casually as she'd asked about what I'd baked for breakfast.

I was still trying to recover when Crystal muttered 'what the...' under her breath. Her eyes were wide and fixed on the wall where Stacey's paintings were displayed.

"Woah. What is that?" I blinked a few times, but the green light shining from the middle of the wall kept getting brighter. When it stretched out into a thin shimmering green line, I got to my feet to take a closer look. By the time I'd made it across the room, the line had stretched and turned downward on both ends, forming two perfect right angles.

It wasn't reassuring to see that the more experienced witches in the room looked as perplexed as me. "What's happening?" I asked anyway.

All three of my friends shook their heads and shrugged. When the line stretched to the ground, they inched closer.

"Is it... a doorway?" I asked, following the shape with my eyes. It was about as tall as a regular door and about twice as wide. As I stared, the glowing lines flared brightly before fading away and blinking out. Hattie almost fell forward when the wall vanished the instant she placed her hand on it.

"What the..." Crystal repeated.

None of us had an answer for her.

TWENTY TWO

The center of the large wall where Stacey's photos usually hung had turned into a large doorway that, without a doubt, had *not* been there a moment ago.

Peering into the dark didn't reveal anything, so I stuck my hand through it and into the cavernous space on the other side.

"What are you doing?" Crystal yelped, grabbing my hand and yanking it back into the bakery. "We have no idea what's in there! What if it's a portal?"

Hattie snickered. "A portal to what? Another dimension? Don't be ridiculous. That's not a thing." She pulled out her phone and flicked on the flashlight, but when she pointed it into the opening, the darkness started to fade as though someone had opened the shutters.

"Woah." Juliette's eyes were wide, and her hand had floated up to cover her open mouth. She'd been standing behind Hattie and me, peering over our shoulders, but she pushed me aside and slipped between the two of us. Without hesitating, she stepped into the large room that had been revealed and turned silently in a circle, taking it all in.

"Is this what I think it is?" Crystal murmured. She stretched her neck forward and peered into the room.

"I think it is." I was having trouble believing my eyes, but for some reason, I was as reluctant as Crystal to step through the opening.

The bakery had taken my breath away when I first saw it. The black and white tiled floors, the bistro tables, and even the antique-style countertop had been plucked straight from my fantasies. There was no doubt in my mind that we were looking at the bookstore of Juliette's dreams.

Built-in cherry wood shelves lined the walls, with a few waist-high ones jutting out at regular intervals to create little nooks. One corner of the room looked perfect for a children's area, and it was easy to imagine cozy seating all around the store for customers who wanted to sample the goods. It was a ridiculous notion, but the empty shelves exuded quiet anticipation, as though they couldn't wait to find out what books they would soon hold.

Juliette stopped spinning so fast, she wobbled in place for a second before looking at us with an anguished expression. "What is happening? What is this place?"

I shrugged and gestured around me. "My best guess? Our building responded to a need or a strong desire."

Her anguish deepened. "But I... This isn't what I want."

Looking past her at the exquisite detail etched into the molding at the top of the built-in shelves, I bit my lip and didn't reply. She might not think this was what she wanted, but I'd never known the building to get anything wrong.

"It's too much. I can't..." I grabbed her arm as she darted through the entrance.

"Hey, you're okay. It's okay. Whatever is freaking you out, we can figure it out."

She shook her head hard and pulled her arm out of my hand. I thought for sure she was going to rush out of the bakery, but she came to a stop before she reached the door.

"I have nowhere to go." Her shoulders slumped forward, and she caved in on herself.

The three of us reached her at the same time, and she let Hattie pull her into her arms. Feeling helpless, I placed my hand on her back. Her body was heaving with silent sobs.

"There you go, let it out. It's not healthy to keep all that inside you," Hattie murmured as I rubbed circles into her back much as I did to Aurie when she was sad.

I was so focused on Juliette that I didn't notice our first customer arrive until the bells over the door jangled.

"Oh, my, Cassie! I didn't know you were thinking of expanding! What a novel idea!" Juliette stiffened under my hand and swallowed a sob. The oblivious customer stepped around our sad little trio and made her way to the counter where Crystal greeted her with a little less exuberance than usual.

Grabbing their coats from the coat hanger, Hattie pointed in the direction of her shop and mouthed that she was going to take Juliette back to her place. I gave my cousin a quick squeeze from behind that she halfheartedly acknowledged with a pat of her hand on mine and pulled the door open for them.

It was probably silly of me to expect her to be thrilled at the thought of a new store, but the depths of her despair made my stomach churn. How was it possible that a new shop would devastate her more than the loss of the original one? It didn't make any sense.

When Hattie and Juliette were out of sight, I joined Crystal behind the counter and leaned against the bread bins, blinking back tears. The customer picked up her latte and wandered away to peer into the new space. My eyes followed her as Crystal came to lean beside me.

"How are you holding up?" Crystal asked.

I half shrugged and scrunched up my face. "Oh, you know. Like someone who ruined her cousin's life by burning down all of her belongings and witnessed that same cousin come undone at the thought of sharing a store."

Crystal grimaced and leaned into my shoulder harder. "It's not your fault, you know that, right?"

"I know in here." I tapped my head. "In here, I'm not so sure," I said, tapping my heart. "If I'd never moved here, Margie's secret wouldn't have been revealed, she would never have started hating me or enlisted Juliette in her run-Cassie-out-of-town campaign. Her quaint little bookshop would still be standing, and Juliette would still have everything she owned."

"Maybe. But Juliette wouldn't know her cousin. She wouldn't have become part of a group of crazy friends. And who's to say Margie wouldn't still have found reasons to torture her?" Crystal said.

I tilted my head and gave her words some thought. "Maybe. And yet." I tapped my heart and grimaced.

"I know. Give it time." She squeezed me again and I rested my head on her shoulder.

My phone pinged, distracting me momentarily. "My dad says they arrived safe and sound at Walden Pond," I said, shoving my phone back into my pocket. That was a relief. I hadn't doubted his ability to drive on snowy roads, but I had wondered how he would handle a bus full of loud pre-teens.

"Oh, that's good news." Crystal hadn't shared my concerns, but she still seemed relieved at the news.

My eyes drifted back to the opening, and I sighed. "And what was that?" I gestured vaguely. "She was more upset today than she was yesterday. I don't get it. It's all such a mess. The building isn't usually wrong, but maybe Juliette doesn't want to rebuild here. Maybe she doesn't want to be so close to me." The thought hurt more than I expected.

"She'll come around. Don't worry. It's just a lot to process."

"Maybe." I wanted Crystal to be right, but deep inside, I wasn't convinced.

Crystal wisely opted to change the subject. "Do we even know who owns that building? It's been empty for so long, I can't remember what it used to be." She frowned as she thought back. "I want to say that at some point it was a fabric store. Or maybe yarn? Something crafty. I think. Like I said, it's been empty a long time."

"It's so weird. It's right next door, but I don't think I ever even noticed it. That's strange, right? I must have passed this building a thousand times since we moved in." Unease made my skin prickle. How could I never have given any thought to a building connected to mine?

Crystal shrugged. "Eh, in a magical town, that's not so weird. There are spells designed to distract people and turn their attention away. Why anyone would have bothered with this place is another question. Either way, it's gorgeous. Maybe the building knows something we don't."

"I have no clue," I replied. "I stopped trying to understand the building's antics a long time ago."

"Do you think it has its own apartment upstairs?" Without waiting for an answer, Crystal darted around the corner and brushed past the curious customer. She vanished from sight and whooped from deep inside the other store. As quickly as she'd disappeared, she reappeared at my side. "There's an identical staircase to yours at the back of the store. It's safe to assume it leads to an apartment too. So cool."

"It's beautiful, and amazing in every way, but this isn't my property. So how does that work?"

"Beats me," Crystal shrugged and patted my shoulder as she turned to greet another customer, "sounds like a question for your little lawyer friend."

TWENTY THREE

W hen my father's text came through, I had to read it three times before the words connected with my brain. Then I sent back a hysterical string of replies that elicited no response, so I did the next logical thing, I texted the Brewhahas.

How they understood my garbled message was beyond me, but within moments, Hattie and Juliette rushed into the bakery with twin looks of concern on their faces. I barely registered their arrival. I couldn't stop reading my father's text, willing it to give me more information, begging it to tell me something different.

> **Aurie didn't make it onto the bus with the other kids. My phone is about to die, but we're on it. The park rangers are on their way. We're going to find her. Don't worry.**

Don't worry. As if I could turn it on and off like that. My baby was lost in the woods, mere days after a blizzard, wearing sub-par winterwear. A blanket of cold dread settled over me. It was a little after three, which meant it would be getting dark in an hour or so. If I got in my car right this second, I could be there with a little daylight to spare.

Crystal was catching Juliette and Hattie up near the espresso machine, and I debated telling them my plan, but I could already hear them telling me to stay put and let the authorities handle it. That would be lunacy. There was no way I could sit by while my kid froze to death, hoping some park ranger found her in the snow-covered forest.

My parka was hanging on the coat rack near the door, and with the bakery closed for the day, there was no one to notice me tiptoeing over, or to notice me use my magic to wrap an extra layer of air around it to muffle any giveaway swish-swish sounds as I took it off the stand. My friends were too intent on what they were discussing to hear me pull open the bakery door.

"I don't know what I'll do if she's somehow behind this too," Juliette's anguished voice reached me as I was pulling the door closed behind me, and as I debated stopping to ask her what she meant, the obvious answer came to me and made me speed up instead. If Aurie was missing because of Margie, she was in more danger than I thought, and the park rangers would be powerless to help her.

My hands were shaking too much to type the coordinates for the lake into the GPS, so I took deep shuddering breaths until my heart slowed down a few beats and my fingers steadied a bit.

40 MINUTES TO DESTINATION

My heart rate picked back up as I pulled the car into traffic. I was going to arrive with barely twenty minutes to spare before the sun went down. That gave me, what, forty minutes before it was completely dark? I could find her in that amount of time, right?

As I wove in and out of traffic and made it to the highway in record time, I sent up a wordless prayer to any ancestral spirits watching over us to do whatever they could to keep Aurie safe. My connection to my great-aunt's spirit was unreliable, so she tended to show up more when it suited her, but reaching out to her couldn't hurt.

Miraculously, the highway was less crowded than usual, and I pulled into the Walden Pond parking lot exactly when the GPS said I would arrive. A quick glance at my phone showed zero bars, and a slew of missed calls I couldn't return. What it didn't tell me was why there wasn't a single park ranger vehicle or police car in the parking lot.

The forest stretching out beyond the parking lot was as serene and beautiful as it had been the last time I'd been here early in the fall, but now there was an added layer of snow dusting the tops of the trees and turning the ground into a shimmering carpet of white. I spied signs of what might have been snow angels in a spot at the edge of the lot and could all too well imagine the kids playing as they waited for the bus to come get them.

The serenity of the nature surrounding me was at odds with my galloping heart. Aurie was lost in those trees, shouldn't I be able to feel some disturbance in the tranquility that reigned here?

I looked around the lot again, double checking to see if maybe there was an offshoot that I hadn't noticed where the Park Rangers had gathered, but I was definitely alone. The hoot of a lone owl in the distance sent a chill down my back. The lack of emergency personnel filled me with dread, but I didn't let myself dwell on the possible reasons for their absence as I pulled my parka on and rummaged in the pockets for gloves and a hat. Maybe there was another parking lot I had overlooked as I pulled into this one.

Once I was as bundled up as possible with the gear I'd found in my coat, I used my air magic to wrap another layer of insulation around myself to keep the worst of the wind away. I made sure to leave my ears free so I could hear Aurie calling for help. The cold stung them as I hurried to the lake trailhead. The class had been going to the pond, right? I mean, why come all the way out here and not go to the water?

I had expected to see signs that the field trip group had come this way, but the wind kept sweeping piled-up snow onto the path obscuring any tracks they might have left behind. It didn't stop me from forging ahead.

The trees in the Walden Pond forest were so dense and tall that it only took a few moments for the parking lot to disappear from view. This was a terrible, terrible idea. I wasn't equipped to search a forest on my own for a little girl. Logic screamed at me to turn back and wait until I could find help. And yet, I kept moving forward. If I found the thick trees oppressive, I couldn't bear to think how Aurie must be feeling.

Hang tight baby girl, Mama is coming.

Every few feet, I stopped and called out for Aurie and paused to listen for a reply, but all I heard was the occasional answering *caw* of a nearby crow. A curious blue jay followed me, hopping from tree to tree until I yelled at him to be helpful and find Aurie for me. At that, he flew off in a huff and left me alone. When I turned back to the path after watching him fly off, it was gone. A pristine blanket of snow dotted with trees that all looked alike surrounded me on all sides. I couldn't even see the footsteps I'd left behind me.

My pulse sped up and I spun around frantically, gasping for air, looking for a sign pointing me in the right direction. Moss. If I could figure out which side of the trees the moss was growing, I'd know which direction I was facing. At least I would if I could remember what that Ranger had taught us when I'd been a kid on a similar outing. Ugh! Why couldn't I ever know anything useful? Not that figuring out which way was north would be helpful, not without having a clue what direction the lake or the parking lot lay.

My breaths were coming so fast I was starting to see spots in front of me. Frozen puffs of air formed a cloud of mist around me, making it even harder to see where I was going. However, staying put—the only other wilderness survival tip I knew—wasn't an option. The temperature was dropping rapidly and, despite my control over the air, my toes and fingers were growing numb. If I stayed still, I'd be hypothermic in minutes.

"AURIE!" I howled at the top of my lungs. If she answered, it would give me a direction to go in. Tilting my head, I put everything I had into listening for a response and my heart leapt into my throat when I heard a faint 'over here' on the wind. "AURIE! WHERE ARE YOU?" I screamed again and paused to listen. The same thready 'over here' came from off to my left, and I picked up my feet and ran.

If she was calling back, it meant she was awake and alert. That was a good sign, right? My thoughts ran wild as I careened through the trees leaping over anything that looked like a root. The next time I called out, I didn't hear anything in reply, and my heart skipped a beat. Had I gone in the wrong direction? Had she lost the ability to answer? Worse, had I imagined the voice?

"AURIE!! Can you hear me?" I shouted, tilting my head back to send my voice as far as possible. It was hard to hear anything over my pounding heart, but a whisper of something reached me from somewhere beyond the trees in front of me.

I hurtled through more trees, cursing how dark it had already gotten, and did my best to avoid the low hanging branches. If I didn't get to Aurie before it got too dark to see, she'd have to spend the night alone in this freezing forest. My breath caught in my throat. There was no way she'd survive. Isn't that how hikers died all the time? They got lost and froze to death because they didn't have the right equipment to weather a sub-zero night?

Ignoring the little voice screaming in my head that I was just as much at risk, I kept running until something grabbed hold of my foot and plucked me right out of the air. A scream lodged itself in my throat as the ground rushed toward my face. A sharp pain shot through my head as it connected with something hard, but it was the snap in my ankle and the bolt of lightning that shot all the way up my leg that took my breath away.

"No. No. No. No," I muttered to myself as soon as I could breathe again. I tried to sit up, but another lance of pain stopped me mid-move, and I fell back into the snow until I could breathe without wanting to throw up.

Cassandra Berry, you are not dying like this alone in the woods. Buck up and get up right this instant! I didn't recognize the voice in my head, but it didn't sound like someone I should ignore. I heaved a deep, shuddering breath, and tried to sit up again. This time, I did my best to not move my ankle at all, but I still lost the ability to breathe a few times on my way up.

Only you would manage to break a bone while trying to rescue someone. This time the voice was undeniably Max, which was concerning since he was very much alive and, as far as I knew, had no telepathic abilities.

I blinked back tears that threatened to freeze on my cheeks and focused on breathing in and out. Staying here until someone rescued me was a death sentence. The wind was picking up and even in the few moments since I'd fallen, a little snow drift had built up against my thigh rendering it numb. If I didn't find some sort of shelter, I was not going to live through the night.

Numb. Snow. The panicked thoughts darting around my head slowed as I focused on the two words. *Numb. Snow.* My ankle throbbed angrily, and pain lanced up my calf when I leaned over to assess the damage. *Numb. Snow.* I slapped my head when the right thoughts finally connected. My hand came away sticky and I peered at it to make out why.

Please let it be sap. Please let it be sap.

It wasn't sap. It was dark enough that I couldn't be sure, but there wasn't a whole lot of flowing sap in the winter, and sap didn't smell so strongly of iron.

I'd been afraid before, but it was nothing compared to the terror that wrapped itself around my chest and squeezed. My head was bleeding, and I was hallucinating my ex-husband, which meant I probably had a concussion, or worse, and I was reasonably sure the bump on the side of my ankle was bone. I was no doctor, but even I knew that didn't bode well for my ability to walk myself out of this forest alive.

A crow *caw*ed at me from his perch high above my head, interrupting a doom spiral of panic. I didn't have Aurie's ability to speak to animals, but he clearly was wondering why I wasn't getting out of the wind.

"Well, Mr. Crow, thank you for asking, but I'm not getting out of the wind, because moving my leg hurts like a mother trucker, and I don't think I can get up without passing out," I called up into the tree.

His answering *caw* wasn't helpful in the least. But the snow he showered on my head when he propelled himself into the sky was.

"Right, snow. Numb," I muttered, leaning forward to pack snow around my throbbing ankle. The cold seeped into my pants and curled itself around my injury, immediately taking the edge off the pain. I was pondering how to keep the snow in place when a particularly biting gust of wind almost knocked me over. "Duh, Cassie. Seriously, you are such a ditz sometimes. It's embarrassing."

The cold combined with a potential concussion made my thoughts sluggish, but I somehow managed to tap into my elemental wind power long enough to wrap it around the snow I'd packed around my ankle to keep it in place. While I was at it, I used a little more magic to bolster my makeshift insulation layer. The relief almost made me sob.

"Right, Cassie. Next step, you have to get up." I put as much positivity as I could muster into my little personal pep talk, but it didn't do much good. After my third attempt to get to my feet, I sank back to the ground with a groan. There was no way I could get up without passing out.

I scooted backward until I was leaning against a tree. "Aurie!" I called again, so she'd at least know she wasn't out here alone, but I didn't have enough energy to project my words far. My pounding head dropped forward as I listened for a reply, but all I heard were the sounds of a forest getting ready for a long, cold night.

Terror pressed down on my chest, making it hard to draw deep breaths. Rocking in place and shivering, I sent out another plea to Bea. I doubted she could get me out of this mess, but I couldn't stand the thought of spending the night alone in these woods. Even the presence of a ghost was better than facing death by myself.

TWENTY FOUR

The cold bit my cheeks, and I blinked my eyes a few times, surprised to find a small layer of snow collecting on my skin. Shaking my head sent a hot red spike of pain through my skull, and I moaned. It was darker than it had been a moment ago. Night was either falling faster than I'd expected or I had blacked out for a bit, which would explain why my magical wind buffer had failed me. The air responded sluggishly when I called to it and the tears that welled in my eyes stung my cold face as they overflowed.

I'll never see Aurie go to the prom. Or walk her down the aisle because Max is doing that over my dead body. Ha, he'll get to do whatever he wants over my dead body sooner than he expected. A sob shook my body, leaving me breathless from the pain shooting up my leg and through my head. The darkening forest around me lurched alarmingly from side to side, forcing me to close my eyes so I wouldn't start throwing up. *Who's going to make her waffles the way she likes? Or bake her favorite birthday cake?* Another sob worked its way up my throat.

Cassandra Berry, you stop that nonsense right this second. My mother's voice inside my head pulled me up short, stemming the flow of self-pity that threatened to overwhelm me. I wanted to argue with her, but I couldn't fight off the weight pressing down on my eyes and mouth. I'd argue later. After I took a tiny rest.

The first thing I saw when I opened my eyes again was the crown molding that lined the walls in *La Baguette Magique!* I didn't usually see it from this angle, mostly because I didn't make a habit of hovering near the ceiling. Everything around me was hazy and shimmery, like I was looking at the bakery through frosted plastic wrap. I shook my head to clear my eyes, but it didn't feel like my head, more like a cloud of particles dispersing in the air.

A lot of weird things had happened since I'd discovered magic was real, but this was on a whole new level. From my vantage point, I could see my friends, huddled together in front of the counter, looking increasingly agitated. Their words were slightly distorted when they reached me, like they were far away, which was weird, because I was floating right above them.

"I cannot believe she'd go off on her own like that!" I'd never seen Hattie more upset and agitated.

"Of course, she went off half-cocked on her own!" Crystal cried throwing her hands in the air. "This is Cassie we're talking about. She's never asked us for help with anything. Why would she start today? Ugh!" She gripped her hair and tugged. "She has no idea what winter is like out here. It would never have occurred to her she needed special gear if she was going to be out after dark."

Amy hovered in the background, shooting Crystal worried glances and wringing her hands.

Juliette looked up from her phone, her eyes shiny with unshed tears. "Either her phone is dead or she's out of range." She paused and visibly sank into herself. "I am so sorry. This is all my fault."

"What are you talking about?" Hattie snapped. "How is Aurie getting lost in the woods your fault? Even if Margie somehow masterminded separating her from the group, I don't see how that makes you responsible."

"I don't know!" Juliette cried. Crystal and Hattie's eyes followed her as she paced. "I should have stood up to her long ago. I should have enlisted Sam's help. Or, I don't know, maybe I should have left well enough alone and kept my distance from Cassie. Bad luck and disaster follow me everywhere I go." She slumped against the counter and dropped her chin onto her chest. "I'm sorry, I don't mean to make this about me. It's just..." She let her sentence trail away and swallowed loudly.

Pushing myself off the ceiling did nothing but disperse me further, which was concerning because it made the scene below me go even more out of focus. The desperate need to be near Juliette warred with self-preservation. I couldn't evaporate, not before I knew everyone would be okay.

"You're wasting your energy." I'd only heard Bea's voice a few times, mostly in my dreams, but there was no doubt the words belonged to my great-aunt. I tore my eyes from the scene below me, letting Hattie and Crystal converge on Juliette to comfort her.

"What's happening? Are you doing this?" I didn't need to look around to know she was hovering next to me.

"You were giving up. You needed a reason to keep fighting. I wanted you to see that they're coming to find you. Your job is to stay alive until they arrive." Her answer made an odd kind of sense, and I didn't question her further. The hint of sadness in her voice should have worried me, but I was too focused on my friends.

"Aw, hon, I'm sorry I snapped at you," Hattie said, giving Juliette an awkward side hug. "These last few days have been a lot. None of this is your fault. For starters, we don't even know if this is Margie's doing. And if it is, that doesn't make it your responsibility. She's a grown-ass woman, let her carry the burden of her evil deeds. We are going to find Aurie, Cassie is going to come home safe and sound, and then we are going to find you an incredible place to live. It's all going to be okay. You'll see."

"She has a place to live!" I cried. *"The building made her an apartment!"* My words floated away unnoticed.

"They can't hear you, sweet one. Don't waste your energy *or you'll miss what matters most."*

The bakery door crashed open letting in a blast of cold air, drawing my attention from Bea. A gasp made the world around me flicker in and out of focus, and, heeding Bea's words, I did what I could to reign in my energy.

"Oh, thank magic you're okay!" Hattie cried, throwing her arms around a bewildered looking Aurie who squirmed out of the embrace to stomp the snow from her boots.

"Of course I'm okay! Why wouldn't I be?" She kicked off her boots, dropped her jacket and gloves on the ground, and rushed over to Crystal. "Aunty Crys, can I please have a hot cocoa with double whip *and* marshmallows?"

Crystal blinked down at her and up at Hugh who was taking the time to knock the snow off his boots outside, rather than inside like Aurie. "What happened? Where's Cassie?"

"How the dickens should I know?" he grumbled. "Make that two hot cocoas please, hold the extra everything. I can doctor it myself." He chuckled and looked around the room at their stricken faces. "What's wrong?"

"Hugh!" Crystal snapped. "You texted, saying Aurie was missing, and we haven't heard a thing from you since!"

"I did no such thing!" he said, looking indignant. The world below me grew blurrier and I cried out as everyone all but faded from my sight. My father's next words sounded distorted and distant. "First of all, I had zero cell reception up there. I don't even know if the text I sent Cass to let her know we'd arrived went through. Second of all, why would I have sent a text saying that? Aurie is very obviously *not* missing." By the time he was done with his sentence, the scene had been replaced by the dark, snowy forest of Walden Pond.

"No! Come back! Don't leave me out here!" My words came out as a hoarse, strangled whisper and all the pain I the movement jarred my head, making me moan, but I couldn't stop myself. "I'm here... I'm in the forest... It's so cold... someone please... help."

"Hush, child, rest..." Bea's words were muted like she was also leaving me, and a wave of panic washed over me, thankfully bringing with it darkness and oblivion.

TWENTY FIVE

"*H*oney, you can't sleep here. You have to wake up,*"* my mother whispered, only it didn't sound like my mother and my mother would never have called me honey. Still, I was so snug under my cozy new comforter, the last thing I wanted to do was wake up.

"So tired, Mama," I mumbled. "Let me sleep."

"I know you're tired, love. I know. But you can't sleep here. If you stay here, you're going to die," my mom insisted. Her tone was a little closer to the one my mother reserved for me when she was exasperated, but it still didn't really sound like her.

"That's so silly," I said, giggling. "How could being in bed be so dangerous?" I reached for my blanket to pull it over my head, but my hand closed around empty air, and when I fumbled around to find it, someone whacked my ankle with a burning hot poker. "OW!" I screamed. My eyes flew open, and I slammed them back shut when my head received an equally painful whack. "What is going on? Mom, what's happening?" I mumbled.

"Honey, I need you to listen to me very carefully." I was wrong, it wasn't my mom. She would have been barking at me by now, not speaking in an even sweeter voice than before.

Even cracking my eyes open a tiny bit sent blinding pain tearing through my head, but something was wrong, and I wasn't going to figure out what by staying under the covers. Why was there so much white? My room was a horrific shade of peach I'd thought looked cool for about a day. And why was my comforter doing such a terrible job of keeping me warm? A violent shiver shook my body and when my ankle shrieked in protest my mind cleared just long enough for the reality of my situation to come crashing down.

"I'm in the forest. Aurie's missing. And I did something to my ankle."

Or maybe I was in bed dreaming this? But that didn't make sense at all. Aurie hadn't been born the last time I slept in that room.

"That's right. You're in the forest and you're hurt. You have to get out of the wind, sweetheart. I can't pull you. You have to wake up enough to move yourself." There was a frustrated edge to the kind voice, and I swiveled my head

to see who was speaking to me. The voice was familiar, and I knew I should have recognized it easily, but I couldn't pinpoint the answer.

"Stop moving, I can't see you. You're too blurry," I mumbled. "Am I drunk? I sound drunk, and my head feels heavy."

"Cassandra!" The blurry shape hovering in flickered into focus almost long enough for my brain to catch up.

"I'm so tired. Imma gonna to close my eyes a few minutes, then I'll see you more clearly." My eyes slid shut, and I slumped back into my bed.

"Cassandra Berry Blackwell, you open your eyes right this minute! Or I'm going to... going to..." Out of curiosity, I kept my eyes shut. What was she going to do? Pull my covers off?

Something tickled the bottom of my foot, and I screamed when my leg twitched in response. "Okay! Okay! I'm awake!" This time, when I blinked, the forest around me was in stark focus, and my terror roared to life and stole the air from my lungs. Bea's shimmering form sagged with relief.

"Oh, thank goodness," she muttered. Her flickering form was soothing, and I watched her shimmer until I could draw a deep breath again. As my fear receded, a nebulous thought wormed its way into my mind.

"Were we just in the bakery together?" I frowned, but the memory stayed fuzzy. "I was... a cloud? That can't be right."

Bea's worried frown deepened, and she cut off my rambling. "*Hon, I know you are very, very cold and your head hurts and you just want to go back to sleep, but I need you to listen to me and I need you to really focus. I am almost out of energy. If you don't do what I tell you right this second, bad things are going to happen.*"

"Bad, like, Aurie not putting her dishes away after breakfast? Because that drives me bonkers." I stopped nodding the instant I started and gripped my head with my hands. "Ow."

"*Cassie, about seven feet behind the tree you're leaning on, there's a hollow tree that is just big enough to hold you. If you scoot yourself there, you'll be out of the wind, and I think you'll be safe until help comes. Please, honey, this is very, very important. There are so many people who would be devastated if you didn't make it home.*" Her voice cracked.

Nothing she said made sense, but I didn't want to be responsible for making her any sadder. "You want me to move to a hollow tree behind me?"

"*Yes! Yes! That's it! It's only a few feet behind you. If you lean to the side, you can even see it.*" She gestured, but seeing the forest through her translucent arm was so distracting,

I didn't turn my head until she growled in frustration. *"Ugh! My kingdom for a corporeal body! Even for five minutes!"*

I giggled. "You want mine? It's a little bit of a mess, but it's yours if you want it." I giggled again. "Silly, Cassie, people can't share bodies," I muttered to myself.

My head was too heavy to turn. It made it about halfway to where Bea was pointing and lolled to the side. Tears pricked my eyes. "I'm sorry," I whispered. "I want to do what you're saying, but I'm so tired."

"That's okay, love. I have an idea. You just close your eyes for a moment and let your old Aunty Bea take care of everything."

I opened my mouth to ask what she was trying to do, but before I could organize the words into a sentence, darkness pressed in from all sides and the words disappeared along with everything else. It was a relief, because as the lights went out, Great Aunt Bea pressed a shimmering hand against my chest, and I could have sworn she started to sink into me. It wasn't as strange as it should have been, which was itself quite disturbing.

"Ugh, that was not a pleasant experience. I will not be doing that again any time soon." I cracked open an eye and watched as Great Aunt Bea shook out her arms. She was more transparent than she'd been before and looked a lot more tired. The trees behind her had changed, or was it one tree now? I couldn't see any light between them anymore. I was warmer than before, but my entire body throbbed with pain.

"Was I in a fight?" I murmured.

"No. Not in a fight. But your body has taken a beating. I'm sorry I wasn't more gentle. It was my first time taking possession of a body. I really hope I didn't do any more damage than was already done. Still, it was worth it. You can't heal someone who's dead."

"You're not making any sense."

"I know. Don't worry about it. It doesn't matter. What matters is that you're safe from the wind now."

"I am?" My head wobbled as I looked around me. The sky and the trees were gone, and I couldn't feel any snow under me. "How did I get here? Where is here? Is Aurie here?" My brain fog cleared long enough for me to remember I was in the forest looking for my daughter, and I pinwheeled my arms to try to get myself upright.

Bea floated over to me and rested a hand on my shoulder. I couldn't feel her, but I still relaxed under her touch. "Remember? We saw Aurie come home. She's safe."

I slumped back down and nodded slightly. "Oh, right. That was real? It felt like a dream."

"It was a little like a dream. It's hard to explain. But she really is home. And now you're in the hollow in the tree I told you about." She shook her head when I opened my mouth. *"It doesn't matter how. It's done. I only have a tiny bit of energy left, and I'm going to use it to find a way to warm you up. You stay put and rest."*

"Wait! Can you show me Aurie again?" My voice cracked and she paused near the small, curved opening I hadn't noticed before and turned back to look at me again.

"I'm sorry, I wish I had enough energy, but I'm all tapped out. Stay alive and you'll see her in person soon." She paused and looked at me with love and longing in her eyes. *"I wish I had lived long enough to get to know you in person. Your daughter and your friends are lucky to have you in their lives."*

Darkness pulled me under before I could figure out why her words sounded so sad.

I didn't think anything of the first scritch, scritch sound that pulled me from a deep sleep. Persimmon was a pretty nocturnal cat, and he often did unexplainable cat things while we slept. The second snapped me wide awake. I wasn't in my bed at home. I was in some animal den in the middle of a forest.

And that animal was coming home.

My heart leapt into my throat and my palms got so sweaty I couldn't get purchase on the dirt floor of the hollow when I tried to push myself upright. A wrong move jostled my ankle and I nearly screamed in pain. Only the fear of being discovered by some rabid animal kept the howl from pushing through my clenched lips.

Oh, crud. Oh, crud. Oh, crud. It's not the cold that's going to get me. It's a bear. Or a bobcat. Or... or... My imagination ran out of big terrifying animals long before reason kicked in. *There are no bears in this park. Also, doubtful that any of the animals here have rabies, and even if they did, they probably aren't looking for cozy burrows to sleep in. Also, this hollow doesn't smell like cat, big or small.*

I took one long slow breath then another and listened. The scratching had been replaced by quiet chittering noises that brought to mind my old pal, Mighty the mouse. That little guy had gotten me out of a tough scrape. Maybe he had friends in this forest that would do the same.

Right, but Mighty was sent to you by Aurie who isn't here to send someone else to help you, so that's probably not what's happening here, is it? My reasonable self was starting to sound a little bit like a know-it-all. I almost missed the confusion that had gripped me earlier.

Fine, if it isn't an animal sent by Aurie, then what is it? Figured that the annoying part of my brain wouldn't have an answer to that.

As quietly as possible, I fumbled around me for something I could use to defend myself if whatever was making its way to me was aggressive and angry about finding me in its bed. Getting the heck out of its hole would have been the better option, but I wasn't going anywhere on my own steam anytime soon. My fingers closed on a medium-sized rock, and I hugged it to my chest. I should have taken my PE teacher more seriously when he told me his boxing tips would come in handy someday.

The chittering stopped, and I held my breath, my eyes glued to the small opening. It was dark both in the burrow and out of it, but with a little luck, I'd get a sense of how big an animal I was going to have to fight.

But when the animals rushed in, I didn't have enough time to process what they were or get into any sort of makeshift fighting stance before they bumped up against me and stopped moving. Twin sets of bright beady eyes focused on me from either side of me and my heart stuttered, then started racing. Whatever animals the eyes belonged to, they stood between me and the entrance to the hollow. Not that I could drag myself out to safety.

"Hi little dudes. Sorry I'm in your house. I hope we can be friends, because I can't move," I crooned in the sing-songy voice. Aurie and I had watched a documentary about training feral dogs and that's how the trainers talked to the terrified ones.

When they didn't move, I took a shuddering breath, then another, and willed my heart to slow down. I was too dark for me to be sure, but it looked like one of the animals cocked its head. Was it debating biting me? Because getting bitten wasn't going to improve my situation at all.

Time stretched endlessly as we stared each other in the eye until I remembered my cell phone. Knowing what kind of animal I was dealing with had to help, right? Moving as slowly as possible, I slipped the hand not gripping the rock into my jacket pocket and pulled it out. Both animals made nervous sounds when I clicked on the light, but they didn't move from their spots on either side of me. My fear evaporated and my heart melted as the light revealed their adorable little faces. I'd never seen a fox up close, and they were a thousand times cuter than I expected.

They must have sensed the tension leave my body because they both relaxed at the same time. One hesitant step at a time, both foxes scootched closer until they were leaning against me. Then, with little happy sighs, they burrowed into me from either side and made themselves comfortable.

Their warmth made me realize how cold I'd gotten. Tucking my phone back into my pocket and making sure my rock was still within reach, I placed a tentative hand on one and then the other, and when neither of them protested, sank my fingers into their fur and let the darkness close in on me again.

TWENTY SIX

Fiery darts of pain shot up my leg and my head throbbed in tune with them, making me groan. Instinctively, I knew that wasn't what had woken me up. If anything, being awake made the pain worse and everything within me begged to be allowed to black out again.

The foxes hadn't moved away, but their heads were up, alert, and focused on the small entrance. I couldn't hear anything, but both animals cocked their heads to the side at the same time.

The urge to whisper 'what is it, Lassie? What is it, girl?' bubbled up, and my snort surprised the foxes. They glanced at me and looked right back at the entrance. That time, I heard the high-pitched scream that had caught their attention. Hope flared deep inside, bringing tears to my eyes and momentarily choking me. Gingerly pushing myself up on my elbows, I held my breath and listened again, but the sound didn't repeat itself. The flash of hope that had given me the momentum to lift myself up evaporated and I crashed back to the ground.

"It's the wind," I whispered, dropping my head against the hollowed-out tree's wall. "It's just the wind." Despair rushed in and a lump formed in my throat. Who was I kidding? It was pitch black in a snowy forest. Who would be crazy enough to risk coming out to find me. And even if someone did, I was hidden deep inside a tree a ways off the path. No one was going to stumble over me in the dark.

The foxes uncurled themselves and moved closer to the entrance to investigate. They didn't look scared, which was reassuring, but something had caught their attention. The bigger of the two pawed at the snow drift that had built up around the entrance.

"Stop that!" I hissed at it. The snow had been blocking the worst of the wind, and without the foxes' warmth, I was already shivering, the last thing I wanted was for it to get colder in my little hideout. I couldn't have slept more than a half hour. Morning was a long way off and if it got any colder, I wasn't going to see it.

The fox completely ignored me and poked its nose out of the small hole it had created. When the smaller fox nudged it out of the way and stuck its nose in the hole, the bigger one made the opening bigger.

"I'm serious! Stop that!" I hissed again. There wasn't a ton of room to move around the hollow, but I was doing what I could to curl away from the wind they'd let in when they glanced at each other and let out the most horrifying scream I had ever heard. The scream that erupted from my throat when my body jerked in response wasn't nearly impressive. But to be fair, the pain in my ankle was so bad it took my breath away, silencing me mid-shout.

If I'd still been screaming, I would never have heard the voice calling to me outside the hollow.

"Cassie! Cassie!" I couldn't be sure, but the voice sounded like it might belong to Juliette.

A gasping sob swelled inside me, further cutting off my ability to breathe. They'd come for me. They hadn't left me out here to freeze all night. All the terror I had been ignoring threatened to swallow me whole. Gasping for breath I tried to respond, but I couldn't get a coherent sound out past the sobs and the tears.

As if speaking for me, the foxes stuck their noses out the hole and chittered loudly.

"Over here!" Another voice called and my sobs grew stronger as I recognized Hattie's voice, then Crystal's, and finally a deeper voice that would have brought me to my knees if I hadn't already been on the ground.

I took a deep slow breath and tried speaking again. "In here! I'm in here!" It came out as a hoarse whisper, but that was enough for the crew outside. Another wave of emotion swelled, bringing with it a fresh onslaught of gasping tears that only increased when the snow drift came crashing into the hollow and revealed Sam's worried face.

He shone a flashlight around the tree hollow and his eyes widened with concern as he looked me over, but he smiled softly when his eyes reached my face. "Hey there. Need a hand?" He grinned, but I'd heard his voice crack, and the tension around his eyes betrayed him.

I was crying too hard to do more than nod and when I cried out and clutched my forehead, his smile faded, revealing fear that only made me cry harder. Maybe it had been the cold, or the shock, or even maybe some kind of self-preserving momentary insanity, but I hadn't realized how scared I'd been. Now I was no longer staring death in the eye, it was like all the terror and the panic were crashing down on me at once, and I couldn't seem to stop shaking.

"She's going into shock. We need to move, fast," Sam called out over his shoulder before looking back at me with his most professional reassuring face in place. It only made me cry harder. "Cassie, you're okay. I promise we're going to get you out of there and take you home. But I need you to take deep, slow breaths. You're hyperventilating and if you keep going, you're going to pass out, and if you do that, I really don't know how we're going to get you out of there." Sam's voice was low and soothing, and he spoke in a cadence I tried to follow with my breath. The first slow intake of air was hard, but the longer he spoke, the easier it got. "Now, I can see that you've injured your head, but does anything else hurt?"

"My ankle," I murmured through my tears. "I think it's broken. There's a weird lump above my ankle and it hurts whenever I move." I waved at the ankle I'd packed in ice. Thanks to the cold, the ice hadn't melted much, and it hurt so much I didn't want to imagine how it would feel if it had.

He dropped his gaze to my leg and uttered a muffled curse before giving me a reassuring smile. "How did you get yourself in there anyway?" His flashlight did a better job of illuminating the space than my phone's light and I was surprised to see that the space was smaller than I'd thought. There would have been room for a few more foxes, but definitely not another human.

"I don't remember," I mumbled, looking around me. The opening was tight enough to make me wonder how the heck I was going to get out. "How am I going to get out if I can't move my leg?"

Sam grinned at me. "Lucky for you, I brought my trusty rescuing-damsels-in-distress-in-the-woods kit which contains an air cast." I tried to chuckle at his joke, but the only thing that came out was a shuddering sob.

The high of hearing and then seeing them all was quickly giving way to the biggest adrenaline crash I'd ever experienced. My whole body started shaking so hard, my teeth were clacking.

"Okay, time to get this show on the road." Sam pulled his head out of the hole and came back, with a shiny rectangular packet. "First things first, let's see if we can warm you up a tiny bit." He unfolded the thin metallic sheet and tossed it over me. "It won't do much, but it'll keep you from losing any more body heat." Once I was covered, he backed up out of the hole, and over the sound of my chattering teeth, I heard him mutter to himself as he rummaged around in his pack. A moment later he was back at the opening with a large plastic contraption. It took him a second to realize there was no way he was going to fit in the hollow with me. He gave me a reassuring smile and backed out. "I'm too big. I can't get in there to put this on her. Who's got the steadiest hands?"

"I'll do it," Juliette said in a shaky voice. Sam murmured a few things to her, then I heard her get onto her knees. "Hey there," she said, poking her head through the hole.

The foxes chittered at her and she said hi back to them, then turned back to me with a grim expression on her face. "Okay, Cass. This is going to hurt like a mother. I mean, like really, really hurt. But once it's on, you're going to feel a million times better and we're going to be able to get you out of here and get you home." The shakiness was gone, replaced by a forced cheeriness that was almost more concerning. But it didn't matter. There was no way my leg could hurt any more than it already did, so there was nothing for me to worry about.

She looked at my leg and closed her eyes tight. I heard her gulp loudly and move her head side to side. Then she opened her eyes and squared her shoulders. "Okay. Let's do this. Ready?"

I wanted to say no, but I clenched my teeth, nodded, and pressed back against the inner wall of the tree.

"Wait!" Sam said from outside. Juliette peered out under her arm and took the thing he handed to her. "Tell her to put this between her teeth."

Juliette's eyes widened, but she handed me the thick piece of rubber and mimed biting down. My fingers brushed against deep grooves in the rubber, but I didn't understand what they were until I put the bite guard in my mouth.

I was wrong. It could hurt more. My teeth bit their own grooves into the thick bite guard when Juliette started maneuvering the air cast under my foot, then thankfully, blackness pulled me under.

Murmured sounds penetrated the fog filling my head and after a few repetitions, what I'd thought were nonsense noises started to make sense.

"You're okay, I've got you. You're okay, I've got you. You're okay, I've got you."

My body was being jostled, but for the first time in hours, pain wasn't coursing through me other than the bite of the icy wind on my cheeks. Something was different about the dark surrounding me and dark shapes slipped in and out of sight, but it took me a moment to realize why I was no longer shivering with cold. Instead of rough bark, my cheek rested against soft flannel, and if I listened carefully, I could hear the rapid thumps of a heart hard at work. My legs were bouncing up and down, but the movement wasn't accompanied with excruciating pain.

"Wheremy?" I mumbled.

"You're okay. You're safe. I've got you." Recognizing Sam's voice as the voice that had been crooning to me, I let myself melt against him. He was warm and so solid and for the first time in hours, I let myself believe I was going to make it through the night.

TWENTY SEVEN

"Wait, I want to know how the rescue played out, but I can't listen to all of you at once!" Collective relief was making everyone in my hospital room giddy and silly and they kept interrupting each other to add what they thought were salient details. Stacey had sent a series of panicked texts and I had promised to share how it had all gone down, but if everyone didn't settle down, I'd never have anything to tell her.

The rush through the woods and to the hospital was a short blur in my mind, but from what I'd been told, Crystal's potion had warmed me up enough that the emergency room doctors had trouble believing I'd been out in the cold for so long. My lower leg had been in bad enough shape to require surgery, but the doctors had assured me the break had been pretty straightforward, and my ankle would be good as new in six weeks or so.

"Okay! Okay! Shush, everyone!" Crystal called over the cacophony. If they didn't settle down, we were all going to get a stern talking to from the shift nurse again. Hattie had somehow convinced her to let them all in with coffee and pastries (I'd have to thank Christina for pulling double duty in the kitchen and Amy for standing by to tend to the early customers) even though visiting hours didn't start until afternoon. If we were too disruptive, she was going to send everyone packing. Luckily, they all listened to Crystal and settled down. "So, it all started when we realized you were gone."

"Please don't ever do that again," Sam interrupted. "I don't think my heart can take it."

I was about to protest, but Crystal narrowed her eyes at me and continued. "We trying to figure out how to find you and stop you from doing something stupid," I opened my mouth, and she quirked an eyebrow at me until I shut it again, "when Hugh and Aurie came home, totally oblivious to what had happened."

"Yeah, Mom! They were all super worried and I was all 'can I have some hot cocoa.' It was hilarious." Aurie caught the looks on everyone's face and hurried to add, "I mean, it wasn't funny anymore after I found out why they were worried." Everyone around the bed laughed, some harder than others, and Aurie blushed and looked down at the bedspread.

I squeezed her hand, and she looked up. "I'm so glad you were never lost in the forest."

"Me too!" She shuddered then perked up. "It was my idea to call Sam. You know, because he loves outdoorsy stuff. And," she smiled coyly, "because he likes you." She drew out the vowel on the word like until both Sam and I were squirming then burst into giggles.

"Right, so Sam arrived and called all his sheriff buddies to tell them to be on the lookout for a crazy old woman wearing bright rainbow clothing, then he helped us gather gear for our heroic rescue. While he did that, Juliette used a spell she'd written," my eyes flew up my forehead and I glanced over at my cousin who was doing her best not to make eye contact with anyone, "to turn one of Amy's amulets into a sort of diving rod attuned to you. It was a really cool bit of magic, actually." Crystal looked suitably impressed and Juliette blushed even harder.

"It's just a small finding spell I've been working on to help me find stuff for my clients," Juliette protested, but no one in the room was fooled. Creating magical objects was a rare talent, one that none of us had ever suspected Juliette of having.

"In any case," Crystal rolled her eyes at Juliette, "the amulet led us right to you."

"No it didn't! It flared out before we found her," Juliette argued.

"Fine," Crystal amended with another eyeroll, "it almost led us to you. The foxes did the rest."

"Foxes that you sent?" I asked Hattie.

She shook her head, looking a little embarrassed. "It wasn't me. I had a bunch of critters out looking for you, but the snow was doing a number on your scent trail and the birds couldn't see you from above."

"But they acted almost tame." I frowned. "It must have been Bea," I muttered almost to myself.

"Bea?" Crystal asked.

I waved my hand dismissively. "Long story that can wait until you're done."

"There's not much more to say, really. The foxes screamed and Hattie understood what they were shouting, and you know what happened next."

"Juliette tried to put my leg an air cast and I passed out like a wuss."

"Not like a wuss," Sam protested. "Like someone nearly in hypothermic shock who was in excruciating pain and somehow held on until she was rescued." He squeezed the hand Aurie wasn't holding and smiled down at me, a lingering trace of horror darkened his usually bright eyes, and I squeezed his hand back to reassure him that I was safe.

"How come I stopped being cold before we got back to the car?"

Crystal brightened, "I made a warming potion! It worked so well, I think we should sell it in the bakery in the winter."

Everyone around the bed nodded enthusiastically and the delight in all their faces brought tears to my eyes.

"I don't know how to thank you all for risking your lives to come save me." I blinked fast to keep my tears from falling, but one escaped and trailed down my face.

Collectively they all shook their heads. Hattie and Crystal also rolled their eyes.

"Don't be silly. That's what family does," Juliette said softly, grabbing my good foot and giving it a little shake. "But there is something you could do for us."

I sat up a little straighter, ready to agree to whatever she suggested, no questions asked. It was the least I could do. "What?"

"Promise you'll never do that again!" they all called out in unison.

I slumped back against my pillows and grinned. "Fine. You win. I promise never to go rescue my daughter alone in the dark woods ever again." I interrupted their answering laughter. "Now go do the things you have to do. Aurie has to get to school, and Crystal and Hattie have stores to open. I need a nap."

"Aye aye, captain." Sam mock saluted me and ushered everyone out of the room.

Juliette paused at the door and looked back at me with a smile. "I'm really glad you're okay."

"I'm glad you're okay, too. This has been a rough week. I hope things calm down after this."

She snorted a laugh in reply and hurried out the door to catch up to the rest of the crew as I sank back into my pillows, basking in the warmth of their love.

TWENTY EIGHT

Heavy footsteps echoed in the empty room, yanking me from my thoughts and making me wobble on my scooter. My eyes flew open and darted around the room until they landed on my father, standing in the opening leading to the bakery with a sheepish expression on his face.

"Didn't mean to startle you. Assumed everyone would be fast asleep. Certainly didn't expect to see you down here."

I gestured to my heavily bandaged leg. "Couldn't get comfortable." One night in the hospital had been all I could take, and I had begged the doctor to let me go home so I could get some sleep in my own bed. But without the machines beeping endlessly and nurses coming to check on me every few hours, I had nothing to distract me from the pain.

"Hhm," he harumphed, coming closer.

"What are you doing down here?" I asked.

"Haven't really had a chance to check this place out what with all the..." He gestured vaguely toward the bakery as he peered inside one of the built-in bookshelves with a grunt. "Good construction, wherever it came from." He jerked his head in my direction. "Think the whole building doing what it wants thing will ever not be weird?"

His question surprised a laugh out of me. "Doubt it."

After everything we'd gone through, being in the new store was even more surreal than it had been after the fire. Even though the shelves were bare, there was no doubt what the building intended for it to be. Little books were painted all around the shop window in a style reminiscent of the pastries painted on the bakery display window. And a large wooden sign carved to look like an open book hung above the door. It was still blank as if the building hadn't wanted to overstep and name the place. Which was hilarious given how much it had overstepped in every other way possible.

"All the chickens are upstairs in the apartment kitchen," Juliette's soft voice startled me, and I jumped.

My father popped up from behind the counter where he'd presumably been examining the workmanship and frowned. "What?"

"Sorry if we woke you," I said with a smile as she stepped softly into the shop.

"You didn't, I couldn't sleep." She didn't elaborate and I let it go.

"Are they really all up there?" I asked instead.

"What chickens?" my father asked.

A soft blush worked its way up her cheeks. "It's dumb. My old bookshop had a little kitchen the previous owners had decorated with chicken figurines in all sizes."

"Like this one?" He gestured to Cluck-Cluck that some-one had placed on one of the higher shelves.

"Yeah, like that one." Juliette smiled. The black chicken with white polka dots looked strangely at home up on his perch.

"And there are more upstairs?" The conversation seemed to be frustrating my father, but he appeared deter-mined to shepherd it to the end.

"Yeah. When we got home from the hospital earlier, Crystal and I explored. She pointed out that I didn't have to live there if I didn't want to, but there was no harm in checking it out."

"And by that, you mean curiosity was driving her to distraction?" I said with a smirk.

"Something like that." Juliette grinned back. "Every-thing is up there."

"What is?" My father frowned at her, and I could almost hear him telling her to hurry up and get to the point.

"Oh. My clothes. And my favorite books. And all the chickens from the shop. To be honest, it's freaking me out a little." Juliette sank gracefully to the ground and crossed her legs. She placed three glass tumblers and a full bottle of whiskey on the ground in front of her.

"It's weird magic. There were things in my apartment that shouldn't have been possible." My father said, eyeing the floor with disdain.

"Like what?" Juliette asked, sounding genuinely curious to hear what had flustered my unflappable father.

"Doesn't matter," he grunted as he attempted to lower himself to the ground.

"Maybe we should move this party next door?" I gestured at the empty bakery behind me. "If I sit down, I don't think I'm ever getting up."

Aborting his awkward maneuver, my dad popped back up, nodding enthusiastically. Looking a little sheepish, Juliette got to her feet and followed us into the other room. Letting the matter of what had taken my father aback in his apartment go, Juliette went back to what she'd been talking about before he interrupted her. "What really confuses me is this. Why the clothes and the chickens, but not the books?"

"I thought you said your favorite books had shown up." I cocked my head at her and frowned.

"Yeah, but none of the bookstore books." She gestured to the empty shelves in the other room.

"Huh." The corners of my father's mouth turned down as he gave her words some thought. "Maybe the building only recreates things that can't be replaced. What's special about those books?"

Juliette blinked at him slowly and nodded. "Well, some are rare editions I found at estate sales. But the truly special ones are the books I'd inherited from my mother. She used to read them to me at night." She squeezed her lips lightly and looked away.

"Well, there you have it." My father shrugged and pulled the bottle toward him.

"You're not as dumb as you look, old man." Her words had their intended effect and the corner of his lip quirked up in a half smile.

My father cracked open the bottle and poured a small amount of the amber liquid into the three tumblers.

I narrowed my eyes at him. "Is that safe for you to drink?"

"Safer than it is for you to question whether or not I should be." He scowled at me and picked up his glass.

"You're one to talk. How many meds did they give you in that place?"

I scrunched up my nose and put down the glass I'd picked up. He was probably right.

He snickered and rolled his eyes. "I was kidding, one sip isn't going to kill you. Live a little, Cass."

I squirmed in my seat and toyed with my glass, but I didn't pick it back up. "Have you given any thought to what you're going to do?" I asked Juliette, partly because I was curious and partly to deflect everyone's attention off me.

She picked up her glass and took a sip, looking between us into the bookshop. Shaking her head, she said, "No. Yes. I don't know."

"Well, that covers it," my father said in his snarkiest tone. He picked up the bottle and despite the warning glance I shot at him, poured himself another glass. I hadn't checked his blood glucose levels in weeks, but if he was being this cavalier with his diabetes, maybe I should start again.

"Don't get me wrong, it's amazing. Exactly the store I would want if I had to design it myself." She stopped talking and kept staring into the empty shop.

"But..." I prompted.

"I can think of a million ways to make it super successful."

"But..." I said again.

She looked at me and shook her head. "But for a glorious afternoon, I was free. For the first time in my life, I have some money in the bank. I could travel, or go to school, or... I don't know, buy a boat and sail around the world."

"You know how to sail?" my father asked, looking surprised.

Juliette hitched her left shoulder and half-smiled. "No, but my father was a sailor. Maybe it's in my blood. I just meant that for the first time in my life, I can make a major life decision based on desire rather than need..." Her voice trailed away and she looked back at the empty space.

"And you feel like the building took that decision away from you," I concluded for her.

She glanced back at me, looking surprised. "Yeah. I guess that's it. How can I walk away from this?" She gestured toward the new shop. "It's the ultimate gift horse and I'm here poking at its molars and hemming and hawing."

"I can't travel and run a bookstore. If I've learned anything over the last few years, it's that owning a store is a full-time endeavor. You know how it is." She looked right at me and tilted her head to the side. I couldn't argue with her logic. Today had been my first day off since we'd opened, and it had been forced on me.

"I could help you run it." The words came out so mumbled, both Juliette and I had to lean forward to hear them. My father lifted his head and repeated himself louder. "I said, I could help you run it. Then you'd be free to come and go as you please."

Juliette frowned. "Do you know anything about running a bookstore?"

"No. Did you when you opened the last one?" The angle of his head said he knew the answer to his question. "Listen, I love living here. I love being near you and Aurie," he said to me, "but I am so bored, I might lose my mind. I've never had so much damn free time on my hands." He held up a hand when he saw me start to reply. "I know you keep saying you need my help in the bakery, but it's obvious I get in the way more than anything. But if I don't try to help, I feel like a mooch." A brief flare of anger lit up his eyes. "But it's not like I can ever get another job trucking. Not with the damn diabetes."

His outburst left me speechless, but Juliette nodded knowingly. For a moment, we all sat in silence, lost in our own thoughts. How had I not noticed what was up with my father? He didn't seem unhappy. If anything, I was a little jealous of all his free time.

"With that nice sitting area, I could organize more book clubs and book signings." Juliette's voice was soft and directed at her empty glass.

"Eh?" My father looked up and blinked a few times as if he'd been far, far away and needed a moment to orient himself.

"Book club. Gatherings in the shop," Juliette repeated.

"You could do demos, for non-fiction books," he suggested.

Juliette perked up. "Yeah! And with the bakery so close, we could do tie-in events. Cassie could bake things related to the books I promote." She directed the last comment in my direction with one eyebrow raised questioningly.

"Totally," I replied. "That would be fun."

"You'll need a big table of sorts. Maybe more counter space." My father pursed his lips and nodded to himself. "Easy enough to make."

"You know your way around wood?" I couldn't help the surprise in my tone.

"Hey," he snapped. "I'm more than just a trucker, you know."

I held up my hands in surrender. "Sorry. I meant no offense."

"We could really do it," Juliette said, ignoring our mini altercation. "We could make this work."

My father raised his chin. "We could, but I don't want to be your employee." Juliette's face fell. "I want to be your partner. Doesn't have to be 50/50, but I want a vested interest. Then maybe I won't feel like such a freeloader."

"I was going to pay you, you know," Juliette said.

He shrugged one shoulder. "This feels better."

My head swung back and forth between them. The stress of the last forty-eight hours and the medication were finally starting to catch up with me and everything felt a little surreal.

Juliette gave his words some thought and then nodded her head once decisively. "You're on. 70/30... And I get to travel whenever I want."

He cocked his head and gave her words some thought. "60/40, and we both get to travel when it works for the other."

They were both grinning like fools as they clasped hands and shook. "Deal," Juliette said.

"Deal," he echoed, holding up his glass to toast our agreement.

"Not to put a wrench in your grand plans, but we still have no idea who owns that building. Maybe we should figure it out before anything gets finalized."

TWENTY NINE

Negotiating the kitchen on a knee scooter was harder than anticipated but with a lot of help from Christina, we got through the morning prep with enough time to enjoy coffee with the Brewhahas. Thanks to the building's magic, everything I needed to get around with my broken leg had been waiting for me when I'd gotten home the previous afternoon. There was a knee scooter both upstairs and downstairs, and much to Aurie's delight, the building had even produced an ancient chair lift in the stairwell.

While Juliette regaled us with details about what the building had materialized for her, I looked around the table at my friends and smiled. She caught my grin and misinterpreted it. "All's well that ends well."

I started to smile back at her and hesitated. "Well, there is still the issue of your grandmother setting fire to your shop and burning down your home."

A twinge of pain made Juliette wince. "But it's all good. I have what matters. And a gorgeous new store. I don't want to think about the rest anymore."

"Juliette! Your grandmother is a menace! She tried to kill me two days ago, she almost killed Aurie last month, she's been torturing me for weeks, and she burned down your store!" I finished on such a shrill note, it made everyone around the table flinch. "Who knows what she's going to do next?" I finished more softly.

"Well, we're going to have to wait to find out like everyone else," Sam said, stepping into the bakery. He'd texted me earlier to say he had things to discuss and to save him a morning bun. My stomach had been doing cartwheels ever since. Seeing him in the flesh turned the cartwheels into triple somersaults. "No one has seen any trace of her. I've had every local agency on the lookout and she's nowhere to be found."

"What about her house?" I asked, frowning. Margie had fought so hard for her place as the town matriarch. She was more the type to hold on to that until her dying breath than to walk away without a fight.

"It's empty. Everything is gone." Sam shrugged. "We'll keep looking, but if she's in the wind, it might take a while to locate her. Until we do, I don't think you have anything to worry about. I doubt she's going to come back here any time soon."

The anxious look that had appeared on Juliette's face during my rant faded away, and she smiled down at me. "See? It's all good."

They all seemed so sure that the danger had moved on, but a flutter in my belly wouldn't allow me to let go of my apprehension. Margie had been making my life so difficult for so long, it was going to take me a long time before I believed she was really out of my hair for good.

"I know. It's just..." They looked at me expectantly, but I couldn't bring myself to voice my lingering concerns. "You know what? Let's talk about something else. Did you tell these two what you and my dad decided last night?" I asked Juliette.

The grin that split Juliette's face made them both sit up.

"You're going to do it? Start over here?" Crystal asked, her eyes bright with excitement.

Juliette nodded, looking more scared than confident. "I think so. We're still working out what that will look like, but I think so."

"We?" Hattie asked, leaning forward.

"Hugh and I are going into business together." A hint of trepidation made Juliette's voice waver.

"Wow! That's exciting" Crystal jumped up and hugged Juliette. "It's going to be so awesome to have you right here."

Juliette looked a little taken aback by Crystal's enthusiasm, but it didn't slow her down. "I know! I have so many ideas for integrated promotions we can run and different ways we can make the two stores support each other. It's going to be so much fun!"

I nursed my coffee while they bantered ideas around and tried to hold on to my joy, but as they got more and more amped up, a niggle of worry wormed its way into my excitement.

"Cass? What do you think?" Crystal finally asked, turning to look at me.

I blinked and shook my head. "Sorry, I'm a little distracted. I have to make a call." They looked on with worried frowns as I struggled to stand up and put my leg back in the knee scooter. "I'm okay, I swear. Just a little tired."

"Do you need a hand getting back upstairs," Crystal asked, glancing at the swinging doors with a concerned expression.

"I'm good. I've been practicing." I smiled as broadly as I could and did my best to not wince from the pain as I scooted away. It was bad enough that I had put everyone in danger by going off into the woods on my own. The last thing I wanted was to be a burden, especially since it would be at least a few days before I could get back to work.

My phone rang as my chair lift made it to the top of the stairs, but I managed to get myself into my upstairs scooter and to the couch before the call was sent to voicemail.

Seeing the lawyer's name on the screen, I settled back into the couch cushions as I tapped 'answer.' I hadn't had many dealings with Mr. Lathrop Jr., but I did know that conversations with him were never short.

"Mr. Lathrop. Hi! Thank you for calling me back so promptly." I had texted him the morning of my Walden Pond ordeal and hadn't expected to hear back from him so soon.

"Of course, Ms. Berry. I would never leave my favorite client waiting. Plus, you know me, I can't ignore a good mystery."

Favorite client was a stretch. We'd only spoken a handful of times since he'd reached out to inform me that I had inherited the bakery from my previously unknown great aunt Bea.

"Did you find something out for us?"

"Actually, I did. Fascinating stuff. Fascinating." His voice faded and I worried for a second that I'd either dropped the call or lost him to his papers.

"Please, tell me more." I leaned my head back against the cushions and closed my eyes.

"Well, I looked through the city archives as you requested in an attempt to find the owners of the building next door, and wouldn't you know it, the building *is* connected to the Blackwell estate."

I positioned the phone better against my ear. "Are you saying the building is... mine?" A flurry of emotions danced in my gut that I didn't want to examine in depth.

"Well, not exactly, per se." He paused and everything inside me stilled. "It appears that, back in the day, when Mrs. Beatrice Blackwell's parents were still alive, they purchased the building next door, presumably to expand their bakery, but when they passed, your great aunt didn't inherit the building. It moved into a separate trust set aside for her brothers. And, as you well know, the younger brother William passed away shortly thereafter, so the trust was left to your grandfather, George."

"But George left Portney and never returned." I was having trouble following the way this was unfolding.

"Correct! But the trust accounted for that and was passed down to George's offspring when he passed. And, interestingly enough, at that point, also shifted to include William's offspring."

"I don't understand. I thought that the birth of Juliette's mother was a well-guarded secret. Are you saying that somehow knew about them?"

"I'm sorry to say I don't have an answer to that. The documents don't list anyone by name, they only mention 'any potential offspring.' Mr. Lathrop sounded apologetic but also a little frustrated. The poor man really hated to leave a mystery unsolved.

"Let me get this straight, are you telling me that my father and my cousin are equal owners of the building attached to my bakery?" My heart leapt with relief.

"Yes! Isn't that fortuitous? The building belongs to two people who already live in Portney! One of whom is already under your roof! Isn't it marvelous? Simply amazing. I do so love it when things work out so neatly."

"Neatly. Yes. That's... amazing." Had the building known? Or was this a complete fluke? Or, even more mind-boggling, had the building's magic somehow reached back in time to orchestrate the whole thing? At this point, that didn't seem all that implausible. The potential permutations made my head spin, and I hurried to thank the attorney and offered to pay him for his time.

"Of course. I'll have my assistant send you the bill, but I'm discounting my hourly rate. I enjoyed myself far too much to accept full compensation for untangling this delicious little mystery." He signed off, leaving me sitting there with my head spinning. For a moment, I'd been terrified I was going to lose my cousin after having just found her. Instead, she was moving into my building, and there was a compelling reason for my father to stay put as well. My heart swelled with joy.

"Crystal? Juliette?" It was mid-morning, so the tables were full of happy customers, but my cousin and partner were nowhere to be seen. Luckily, no one was in line waiting to be served.

The text I had shot off to Juliette and my father as soon as I got off the phone with the lawyer was still unread. I'd spent an hour tormenting myself by imagining a list of the possible bakery-related disasters that were keeping them from their phones before giving in to my curiosity and making my way back downstairs.

The doctors had told me to take it easy for a few days, which Crystal had interpreted as 'don't let Cassie work for three days,' but they hadn't said anything about not hanging out with other people. Anything was better than sitting up here wondering how my bakery was faring without me.

"They're in there," one of our more frequent regulars said, pointing to the opening between the two shops.

"Come get a load of this!" Crystal called.

The reason for her excitement became clear before I had scooted myself all the way through the bakery. A precarious tower of boxes leaned against the counter and Juliette and Crystal were kneeling in front of two open boxes, rifling through their contents.

"What's all this?" I frowned, trying to make sense of what I was seeing.

Juliette popped her head from around one of the boxes, her eyes bright with excitement. "Books! It's all books! Can you believe it?" She was smiling even as she blinked back sudden tears. "Sean just showed up out of the blue. It seems that he's been spreading the word asking people to donate gently used books to get me started. He already has a dozen boxes for me!"

My question about who Sean was died on my lips when the EMT who'd patched Juliette up after the fire set down two more boxes next to the ones already stacked near the counter and grinned at me. "Isn't it incredible?"

At the time, I'd been too overwhelmed to notice, but he's kind of cute in a 'boy-next door' way. From the smile on Juliette's face, it's obvious she already knew.

"Incredible, for sure." My head spun at the speed with which things were developing,

A loud bang from the corner of the store made me jump.

"Is that my dad?" I asked Juliette, probably sounding as bewildered as I felt. He was kneeling in the middle of stacks of wood, happily hammering away.

"He's building a community table! It's going to be gorgeous." She clapped her hands happily.

"He really knows how to build things?" In my mind, my father has spent the last forty years sitting in the cab of a truck. But that was silly. Even so, it was hard for me to picture him doing anything else. Even harder to picture him with a hammer in his hand. Who had he built things for?

"I guess so!" She shrugged and turned back to Sean who was asking if she wanted help unboxing the books.

"What do you think, Cassie? I should probably wait until I have the equipment to catalog them, right?" Waiting looked like the last thing she wanted to be doing.

"It can't hurt to unbox them. You can always log them when you're shelving them." I shifted uncomfortably on my scooter. "But before you start, there's something I need to discuss with you and my dad. If we could do it sitting down, that would be fantastic."

THIRTY

With everyone and their nephew stopping by to pitch in, getting the new bookstore organized and ready for the grand opening was like one long continuous party. People streamed through the bakery to the bookstore and back again and the energy in the air was contagious. Future customers dropped by daily to donate more books or to request Juliette carry their favorite author in the store. They inevitably ended up staying to put a few books on shelves, unbox things for the children's corner, or help put together furniture.

Having so many hands to help was incredible, but it did mean everyone had an opinion about something. My father was quick to put them all in their place the instant he decided they were overstepping, so pretty much as soon as they opened their mouths.

He was gaining a reputation as the town grump which, much to his chagrin, was drawing senior ladies to him like moths to a flame. I caught him humming to himself as he puttered around the store, so I wasn't entirely convinced he hated it as much as he pretended.

"Anyone need a cup of coffee in there?" I asked, rolling over to the opening between the two stores. Half of the morning's helpers yelled back their orders and I called them back to Crystal.

Juliette had confided in me that she had underestimated how nice it would be to have a bustling bakery pretty much inside the store. She loved the mouth-watering smells that were always circulating and didn't even mind the constant happy hubbub of chatter. Secretly, despite the way she lamented the peace she'd enjoyed in her last store, I thought she was enjoying the background noise.

Any misgivings I might have had about the bookstore vanished the moment I saw how happy my father was with an outlet for all his pent-up energy. Juliette's obvious delight was icing on the cake.

"Hey, cuz? Can I get you anything while I'm at it?" She glanced up from the computer screen and shook her head.

"I'm fully caffeinated, thanks! Any more and these spreadsheet lines are going to be illegible," she replied with a grin.

Unlike her old store, the counter in this store was an island in the middle of the shop, which meant she had a 360 view of the inside, could look through into the bakery, and could see out into the street. From where I was standing, I could also see outside, so we both had a clear view of the person peering through the window into the store with a dark scowl on her face.

My perfect bubble of joy popped, and reality stole my breath as it rushed in. The world around me lost some of its light, and the happy noises I'd been enjoying a moment ago suddenly grated on my nerves. My lip curled up and rage made my hands shake. A quick glance at Juliette revealed that she'd had a very different reaction. Her shoulders were curled forward, and she was cupping her stomach with her hands. I'd never seen her look paler.

No one else in the room had noticed a change—most likely because they hadn't looked up from their respective tasks—and a protectiveness that was as strong, but somehow different than the one I felt for Aurie rose up inside me and lent me the strength I needed to finally face the one person who kept threatening my happiness.

Juliette glanced at me and met my unwavering gaze. Emotions flashed too quickly through her eyes for me to interpret them all, but the mix of guilt and resignation that dominated only stoked my anger.

I should have picked up my phone and called Sam right then and there. That would have been the smart and responsible thing to do. But I needed to look her in the eye and ask her why she so desperately needed to ruin my life. As a concession to my moral conscience, I selected Sam's name on my phone so it would only take a single tap to call him.

By the time I'd started navigating my knee scooter toward the bookshop entrance, Juliette was slipping on a sweater and murmuring something about going outside for a bit of fresh air. If anyone noticed us maneuver the scooter through the door and slip outside together, they didn't mention it.

Within moments, I was outside shoving my face in Margie's while Juliette grabbed her by the elbow to keep her from darting away.

"What are you doing here?" I hissed, as Juliette shepherded her away from the window where anyone could see us.

If she was taken aback by my forcefulness, she recovered quickly, but she let Juliette lead her to the small alley that ran down the far side of Hattie's pet shop. I trailed behind them, avoiding the worst of the slushy puddles, shooting furtive glances around me. The instant we were hidden from view, Margie shook Juliette's hand off and straightened up until she was looking down at the both of us.

On a good day, I was about the same size as her, but the scooter made it hard to stand tall. Still I was glad to see Juliette staring her straight in the eye. Margie glared at us and waved a hand in the air. Pressure pushed down on my shoulders, like the air around me had suddenly grown heavy. The more I resisted, the harder the pressure got. I resisted as long as I could, but I finally let myself droop over my handlebars. A moment after me, Juliette's shoulders slumped forward under the pressure.

"Better," Margie snapped. The pressure didn't let up. If anything, it only got harder and didn't let up until I finally grunted from the crushing weight. In an impressive show of strength, or maybe an untapped streak of defiance, Juliette never uttered a sound. Knowing full well she'd only flex her power over me again if I straightened up, I stayed hunched over and tapped call on my phone before shoving it to the bottom of my pocket.

"Whatever you want, you should tell us before someone notices we're missing," There must have been still too much insubordination in my tone because the pressure returned with a vengeance. If it hadn't been for the scooter holding me up, I'm sure she wouldn't have let up until I was face down in the murky snow. With a dismissive sneer, she turned her attention to Juliette and grabbed her arm in a more painful version of what Juliette had done to her a moment earlier.

"You think you're so special with your shiny new store, don't you? That I no longer have any power over you because you're no longer under my roof. You couldn't be more wrong." She tightened her grip and twisted Juliette's arm until she cried out, then Margie pulled her closer until their noses were almost touching.

My stomach thrashed when the acrid taste of pure evil filled my mouth. There was only one explanation for it. My eyes widened of their own volition, and I gasped, pulling her attention away from Juliette's horrified face.

"You..." I gagged on the smell. "You've been using dark magic. That's why your plants all died. It had nothing to do with the Rule of Thirds!"

Pride flashed in her eyes, and her grip tightened on Juliette's arm. "Maybe you're smarter than you look after all. Is that how you've convinced my stupid granddaughter that you're happy to share your store with her? I've seen how you look at her. You can't wait for her to leave so you can have that whole space to yourself." Uncertainty flickered across Juliette's face, and she glanced at me with hurt in her eyes.

"Is that true, Cassie?" Doubt wrinkled her forehead and rage made me want to throw things at Margie. Maybe, for a moment, when the store had first appeared and Juliette had wanted nothing to do with it, I had briefly considered using the space for my catering business. But the thought hadn't crossed my mind since Juliette and my dad had decided to open the bookstore together.

Some of my thoughts must have shown in my expression because Juliette's face fell, and the bitter taste of betrayal filled my mouth.

"Of course, it's not true!" I protested, but her expression didn't change, and neither did the taste in my mouth.

A sly smirk twisted up Margie's mouth as my thoughts spiraled and an evil glint filled her eyes like she could hear my thoughts unravel and panic take hold. She may well have, for all I knew. She'd never confirmed or denied her ability to read minds. I couldn't tell if her smile wavered, or if I imagined it when I strengthened my mental shield. I made it as strong as possible, just in case.

I was so focused on my thoughts that I never saw her leg lash out and connect with my scooter. The front wheel slid to the side, unbalancing me as it skidded over a patch of ice. For a moment, I thought I'd be able to stay upright, but when she threw herself against me, my good foot slipped out from under me, and I crashed into a dirty slush puddle. With a sneer in my direction, she grabbed Juliette's arm and yanked her further into the alley.

I watched her out of the corner of my eye, as I struggled to get back to my feet. If she got too far away, Sam wouldn't be able to hear anything she said. She was too arrogant not to say something incriminating, but it wouldn't matter if I didn't somehow get her on tape.

"What the..?" my voice trailed away as I noticed her snake her hand into a hidden pocket and pull out a small vial filled with a murky, swirling dark green liquid. Even from a distance, I could tell whatever it contained was evil. Juliette shuddered when Margie shoved the vial into her hand. They were too far down the alley for me to hear what Margie hissed at Juliette, but the angry scowl on her face didn't bode well for anyone.

My scooter had fallen over, and I was still trying to get it upright when I heard Juliette cry out.

"Yes you, will!" Margie growled. Abandoning the scooter, I dragged myself closer, inching through the muck until I could hear her clearly. Moving slowly so she wouldn't notice me, I eased my phone out of my pocket and angled the microphone in her direction.

"No!" Juliette cried again, shoving the vial back into her grandmother's hand and jumping out of reach when Margie tried to force it back on her. "I'm not doing that. I don't even want to know what's in that vial."

Malevolence rolled off Margie in waves, and I involuntarily shrank back against the alley wall when she stepped menacingly closer to Juliette. "Oh, but you will. And you want to know why?" she hissed, her face inches from her granddaughters.

She waited for an answer, and after a few beats, Juliette caved and asked, "Why? What makes you so sure I'll do it?"

Pleased with her tiny victory over her granddaughter, Margie preened and shot her a smile devoid of any humanity. "You're going to do it, or I'm going to take the entirety of this vial and make sure that little upstart's spawn and her stupid dog drink every last drop of it." Her voice became more intense when a dubious frown crossed Juliette's face. "Don't think for one second that I wouldn't. You know better."

Her eyes flashed as she shoved the vial in Juliette's hand with a textbook cackle, and I saw the moment every doubt Juliette ever had about her grandmother vanished. The taste of her acceptance and understanding rolling across my tongue was surprisingly gratifying.

Juliette straightened up and took a step closer to her grandmother. For the first time, I saw the old woman cower in the face of the younger one.

"For years, I have given you the benefit of the doubt." Juliette's voice wasn't angry or resigned, it was calm and confident. "I have come up with countless excuses for why you're always so angry, always conniving. I have always believed you were just misunderstood, and I did everything I could to make excuses for your attitude and behavior. I felt sorry for you because your life was so difficult." Horror and disgust twisted up Margie's face, but she didn't interrupt Juliette or look away. "But I was mistaken. There is something wrong with you, something truly evil. I don't know if you were born that way, or if you've become twisted because you let in so much darkness over the years that it has smothered any light you ever contained. But it doesn't change who you are today. I hope you rot in jail and then in hell for everything you've ever done."

Juliette was formidable and watching Margie shrink in front of her was so much more satisfying than if I'd been the one finally putting her in her place.

My cousin's eye flickered toward the entrance of the alley and I glanced over in time to see a familiar shadow retreat. With a calculated sneer, Juliette looked down at her grandmother. "Let me guess, your little vial contained something that would make Cassie ill?"

Margie reacted exactly the way Juliette had assumed she would. She puffed herself up and spat on the ground. "Pfft. As if I'd do the same thing twice." She patted her hair and wiggled her shoulders proudly. "That potion will make her customers ill. Her reputation will finally be in tatters, and Portney will at long last be free of her."

My breath caught and I covered my open mouth. If this didn't end the way I hoped and she managed to carry out her plan successfully, I'd be ruined. Despite her best intentions, Juliette's eyes widened in shock at her grandmother's audacity.

"And don't think I don't have a backup plan if you fail me again. Or that I don't have a way to incriminate you. You know I have an in with the DA. That woman doesn't say 'boo' without my say-so."

The relief that flooded me when the familiar shadow popped up again on the alley wall obliterated the image of my customers rolling around the floor in agony.

Margie's gaze narrowed when Juliette noticed the shadow and she glanced over her shoulder.

"No!" she howled, before throwing her hands in the air and muttering something under her breath. I had no idea what spell she was casting, but I couldn't let her get away again, I had too much to lose if she did. The alley we had ended up in didn't lead anywhere, so it was littered with debris no one had ever bothered to clean up. A medium sized stick lay just out of my reach. Stretching as far as I could, I fumbled for it. The instant my hand closed around it, I threw it as hard as I could at her. She didn't even flinch when the stick clattered to the ground a foot away from her. She did when Juliette picked it up and whacked her across the shoulder with it.

Margie rounded on Juliette, one hand raised as it to slap her, but before her arm could come down, Sam threw a glass vial that shattered at her feet releasing a pale pink cloud of dust.

"Margaret Warren, you're under arrest for the attempted murder of Cassandra Berry. Put your hands where I can see them and turn around slowly!"

"What is that?" she shrieked, batting at the particles as they settled on her.

"Nothing to worry about, just a little layer of protection," he said in a soothing tone.

She snapped her fingers and shrieked when nothing happened. Her scream intensified when she flicked her fingers at Sam with no result, and Sam grinned at me over her shoulder. The tension holding me up vanished, and I collapsed back into the slush with relief. Only the thought of washing the muck out of my hair kept me from going all the way down.

We had only been 90% sure the potion Crystal had cooked up to disconnect Margie from her powers would work. The potion required a rare ingredient that was hard to source, but by chance, she had just enough on hand to make one batch. Not having enough to test the potion on one of us had worried me, but we didn't have a choice. We had all agreed that it made the most sense for Sam to carry it with him. He had made us all promise to keep our phones on us and to call him the instant any of us spotted Margie. Every day Sam carried around the vial without using it had potentially decreased the potency, and my confidence in our plan.

A deputy I didn't know nearly as well as Sam stepped into the alley and snapped a set of handcuffs around Margie's wrists and recited her rights. Ignoring him, she turned as he started to drag her away.

"You... You...," she hissed at me. "You think you can mess with me? And you," she spat at Juliette, "you think you can turn your back on family and not pay the price? I'll show you. I'll show you both!"

Anger propelled Juliette forward until she was inches away from her grandmother. "That's where you're wrong," she said, cold fury kept her voice steady and low. "I won't see. Neither will Cassie. You're going away for so long, you'll never set eyes on either of us ever again. And, even if we ever do cross paths, it won't matter. From this moment forward, you are no longer my family." Margie's eyes widened in shock. "We may share blood, but that no longer means anything. I'm lucky enough to have found a family that shows up for me and wants what's best for me, not what's best for themselves. You are nothing to me. No, you are less than nothing. You are a sad, pathetic, angry old lady, and you no longer scare me."

With that, she turned her back on her grandmother and hurried to help me to my feet. Neither of us watched as the deputy turned the corner and took Margie from our sight. As if by magic, Sam appeared at my side and grabbed my other arm. Once I was precariously balanced on one foot, he pulled me into his arms and hugged me close, but I wriggled out of his embrace.

"Did you get the whole thing on tape?"

"Yep." He nodded and held up his phone. "It's all recorded. Every damning thing she said. And I got the DA to agree to a change in jurisdiction, there's no fear she has anything on the DA there. Hattie says she has the Witch Council on standby, so I think it's safe to say it's over."

"Well, I'll believe it when they confirm her powers are bound." I said, shivering. The Brewhahas had explained to me that the same witch council that kept track of people with unique or rare powers could also be called on to punish criminal witches. As Margie had proven time and time again, we couldn't rely on the mundane penal system to put her away.

"You were incredible. Amazing. A force to be reckoned with." Despite the blush blooming on Juliette's face, I kept going. "I have never been more proud to call you cousin." I squeezed her hand and smiled. "Now can I please go take a shower? I am so tired of being cold."

Juliette laughed and wheeled my scooter over. "I think we can make that happen." She turned to Sam. "You coming? I'm sure we can coerce Crystal into making us some celebratory drinks."

"I'll be right in. Just want to make sure she gets where she needs to go. You two go ahead." He tipped his hat at us with a grin and sauntered away like he hadn't finally put an end to our joint nightmare.

"You okay," I asked Juliette as we started to make our way back to our store.

She paused for a second and then nodded. "I think I am. I think my future just got a whole lot brighter, and it's not only a little bit due to you."

"Well," I grinned at her. "My future is brighter because of you, so I guess we're even."

THIRTY ONE

Navigating around the waiting customers to bring Juliette and Amy liquid sustenance in the form of magic spiked lattes was challenging enough to confirm what we'd been hearing all morning from our end of the building. After coming close to hitting a customer with the tray rigged on the front of my scooter, I resorted to chanting 'coming through' loudly as I moved through the bustling crowd. The grand opening of *Wyrd Words* was a raging success and, guessing from the goofy grin plastered on her face, my cousin was having a little trouble taking it all in.

In exchange for a small corner of the store where she could display her jewelry, Amy had agreed to help out in the bookshop whenever she was needed. But given the size of the crowd I had to push through to hand over her coffee, I had a feeling she was going to be needing her own place sooner rather than later. She took the cup I proffered with a grateful smile and turned her attention back to a customer asking how she imbued her pendants with magic. The pride in her voice sent a little flutter of joy through my chest. How far she had come in such a short time.

I waited for Juliette to lift up the hinged portion of the counter that let people in and out of the island and scooted myself inside. "Coffee?"

She beamed at the customer who had just paid and handed her a paper bag overflowing with books. "Have a wonderful day! I can't wait to hear what you think of that shifter series." She woman grinned back and headed through the archway into the bakery. Juliette turned her smile on me. "Another happy customer off to top off her morning with something delectable from your store." She took the coffee I handed her and sighed happily. "Mmmm coffee. How did you guess?"

I glanced at the winding line inside my bakery and quirked an eyebrow. "No idea." We laughed at the same time, and I gave myself a moment to bask in the joy of the moment. "This is good, right?" I was thrilled with how things had unfolded, but a tiny part of me couldn't help wondering if Juliette missed her original store.

"Are you kidding? This is beyond good. It's everything I loved in my old shop and everything I was missing there." She put her cup down and grabbed my hands. "Cassie, I don't think I could be any happier. One of these days, I'm going to find that fortune teller and I'm going to let her know just how right she was when she said I had a big family in my future." She pulled me into a tight squeeze and released me. "Now git. I have work to do. We can't all sit around slacking all day." She winked at me and turned her attention to the next customer in line.

"Oh! Miss Sadie! I didn't know you had it in you," she teased the sweetest older woman in town.

I glanced at the book she was slipping into a bag as Miss Sadie blushed and snickered at the scantily clad Scotsman on the cover. I hadn't figured Miss Sadie for a bodice ripper kind of reader.

Still chuckling to myself, I navigated my knee scooter around a group of teen girls gushing about a new vampire book that looked thoroughly too mature for them and would have rolled right into a table if strong arms hadn't pulled me out of the way.

"Oh! Thanks! I guess I still don't know the layout very well." I smiled up at my rescuer and my heart stilled and then melted. "Hi." I said in a much softer voice.

"Hi yourself," Sam replied, his blue eyes boring into mine. "I guess the opening is going well."

I snorted a laugh as he pulled me out of the way of another enthusiastic book hunter. "You could say that." I grabbed his hand and pulled him into a quiet corner of the bookstore. "It's a little calmer over here."

Peering over my head he read out loud "Local Witch Lore and History? Really?" He laughed. "Not as popular as expected, eh?"

I shrugged. "Juliette knows her stuff. If she made room for it, she knows people want it." I glanced around the bustling store. "Maybe just not this crowd."

When I looked back around, Sam's face was inches from mine and his arms were wrapping themselves around me. "I'm glad you're okay, Cassie." He pulled me against him and hugged me closely. I only hesitated a moment before snaking my arms around his waist. All my internal organs did jumping jacks of joy in response.

"I'm glad I'm okay too, but you know I've been okay for a couple weeks, right?" I teased. My frozen forest ordeal wasn't exactly forgotten, but the initial shock of it had worn off and while I wasn't going to go hang out in the woods by myself again any time soon, I wasn't having nightmares about it anymore. I was even considering giving in to Aurie's increasingly frequent demands to go meet my fox friends.

"I know," he said, squeezing me closer. "But it's going to take me a while before I can get that image of you out of my head."

"Is there anything I can do to help?" It was a genuine question. While I had lived the ordeal, I thankfully remembered little of it, and I didn't have any traumatizing visions painted on the back of my eyelids.

The corners of his eyes creased as a grin split his face. "I can think of a few things," he drawled.

"Oh, yes? And what might those be, deputy?" I teased, resting my chin on his chest and looking up at him.

"Go out with me again." The sudden intensity in his gaze made my insides flutter. "I know you said you needed more time and you wanted to be able to focus on your family, and I get that. I really do. So, if you need it to be just as friends for now, I can," he gulped, "I can make that work. But I want to spend more time with you, not less."

Every part of me froze as I read in his eyes how much this meant to him, and the echoing desire rose up in me.

"I almost lost you, Cass," he continued before I could figure out what I wanted to say. "When I looked into that tree hollow, I thought..." he glanced away, but not before I saw his eyes shimmer with unshed tears that he blinked away before looking back down at me and smiling. "Never mind what I thought. What matters is that I didn't lose you before we got a chance to explore whatever this might be, and I..."

I never let him finish his sentence. Pushing myself as tall as possible on my one good leg, I tucked a hand behind his head and brought his mouth to mine. And when our lips met, I could have sworn I heard an old lady murmur "it's about damn time" off to the side, but I was too distracted by the softness of Sam's lips and the passion in his answering kiss to see who'd said it.

THIRTY TWO

Juliette

"Sh! She's coming!" Aurie shrieked, defeating the purpose of her message. Something in her voice made me want to grin, but her words made my insecurity flare. What had they been discussing that they didn't want me to overhear?

Stop it, Juliette. They love you. Remember?

My rational voice was probably right, but my heart was still in my throat as I knocked. Because this had been presented as a formal invitation—on handwritten cards penned by Aurie that bore a few smears of what I strongly suspected might be dog slobber—I had opted to use the more formal door on the outdoor landing rather than let myself in via the bakery kitchen entrance. To be fair, since the building had helpfully added an outdoor landing to my apartment that connected my door to theirs, this was also the easier way to come. But not the warmest.

I shifted from foot to foot and wished I'd grabbed a jacket before heading over. The door swung open as I was about to knock a second time and Aurie shrieked "SURPRISE!" as she threw the door open. A much larger crowd than I had expected laughed in response, and my heart sped up.

Crowds didn't freak me out as much as they had in the past, but they still tended to make me uncomfortable, especially when I didn't have time to psych myself up beforehand.

Aurie's excitement overrode my urge to run back to my apartment, and the smile I flashed at her was genuine, my cheery tone slightly less so. "Now, that's what I call a greeting! What's the occasion?"

Bouncing on her toes, Aurie slipped her hand into mine and tugged me into the room. "Duh, it's your birthday!"

Her words froze me in place, and she looked over at me with a worried frown. "Are you okay Aunt Juliette? Did we get the date wrong?" Her eyes widened and she looked around frantically for her mother. I pulled my shoulders back into place and took a subtle breath as I patted her hand.

"You didn't get the date wrong. This is an awesome surprise."

Aurie beamed at me and bounced away as Cassie walked over and handed me a glass of something fizzy. "Happy birthday, Cuz."

"How did," I pulled back and looked around the room, my eyes landing on some of my favorite people in Portney as well as a few unexpected faces. Recognizing the people in the room made breathing easier. "How did you know?"

Cassie shrugged. "I have my ways." Her eyes twinkled as she winked at me and stepped away to give Crystal a chance to hug me.

Like they had been coached beforehand, or more as if they knew me well enough to know how much I'd hate it, which was almost too hard to comprehend, no one crowded me, choosing instead to come to me one at a time.

Before I knew it, I had a second glass of the delightful fizzy peach drink in one hand and a half-empty plate of assorted miniature savory pastries on the coffee table in front of me, enjoying the most wonderful birthday party I'd ever had.

The *only* wonderful birthday party I'd ever had.

Before my mother died, we never had money for a party, not that any of the kids in town would have come. After, there was no one who cared enough. By the time I was living on my own, the thought of inviting people over to celebrate me seemed preposterous.

It was hard for me to wrap my brain around it, but no one in attendance appeared put-out to be milling around Cassie's apartment. Drinks and food hand, they were chatting with each other and generally having fun. Instead, I got the impression everyone was genuinely thrilled to be there, and not just because of the food.

Hattie had just enthusiastically sung me an off-key, slightly raunchy version of the happy birthday song and sauntered off to get herself another drink. I was contemplating which pastry to eat next when the cushion next to me dipped under the weight of a new arrival.

Anxiety wasn't the reason my heart started racing when I turned my head to see who had joined me on the couch. The smile that appeared on my face wasn't forced at all.

The corners of Sean's eyes crinkled with delight when my gaze met his. "Happy birthday, Juliette."

"Thank you," I replied, hoping I was suddenly hot because the heat had gone up and not because I was blushing. Somehow, I doubted I was right. "I didn't expect to see you here tonight." Not that I'd expected to see anyone other than Cassie and her family, but still.

"Cassie ran into me at the market last week and asked if I'd like to come," he said with a little sheepish shrug.

"And you couldn't think of anything better to do?" I teased.

"Nope," he replied, and somehow, I didn't think he was joking. "I've actually been meaning to stop by, but things have been crazy at work. How's the store going?"

After getting the book donation train going, Sean had stopped coming around, leaving me to wonder if I'd imagined the attraction building between us. It had taken me a few weeks to shrug it off, but I couldn't forget his warm smile or the way seeing him made me feel. I had briefly considered hunting him down, and just as quickly talked myself out of it. If he wanted to see me, he knew where I worked. The fact that he hadn't come around left little doubt in my mind that he just wasn't that interested in me.

"It's going really well, especially thanks to you," I smiled and did my best to ignore the way his smile caused my belly to flutter. Acting cool and collected seemed so much easier when I played out potential scenarios in my head. Sean didn't smell half as good in my mind as he did in real life.

Take it down a notch, Juliette. He's not into you, remember?

"I'm so glad to hear that." He fiddled with his glass. "Really glad. There's actually something else I wanted to ask you now that things have, ah, settled down." My heart leapt as my mind raced through a list of things he could potentially want to ask me. "I was, ah, wondering if you might like to go to dinner with me sometime. Soon."

This was the question I'd most often imagined him asking me, and I had a dozen answers lined up. The one that popped out wasn't on the list.

"Oh. I assumed you weren't interested," I blurted out, blushing harder than ever when his eyes widened in surprise. "I'm sorry. That was rude."

"No! It wasn't! I was interested." He grimaced. "I was trying to not be pushy. You were going through a lot. I wanted to give you space to process."

The last thing I expected was for my eyes to fill with tears, but I found myself blinking a few away. "That is so... thoughtful. Thank you. As for a date..." I hesitated, the words 'yes! Yes, please! Can we go today?' on the tip of my tongue. His bright blue eyes were wide with anticipation and suddenly, I pictured him looking annoyed at me, and my heart sank. It would crush me when he got to know the real me and walked away and I didn't think I could stand it. I'd be better off not risking it at all. "I don't... I don't think that's a good idea."

Sean's face fell and a confused frown appeared on his forehead. "Oh. I'm sorry. I thought..." he stammered, "I was under the impression..." He jumped to his feet and took a step back, bumping into the coffee table and almost falling over. "I... I should go."

"What was that about?" Cassie asked, watching him dart to the other side of the room.

I sighed. "It was nothing."

"It didn't look like nothing," she said, shooting questions at me with her eyes. "Did he say something rude?"

"Oh, no." I chuckled. Her curious expression was morphing into a concerned one, and I relented. I was still getting used to being able to trust the people around me, but I was getting better at letting down my guard around Cassie and the other Brewhahas.

Look at you, Juliette. A whole group of friends to call your own. Sarcasm had been my last guardian's weapon of choice and her snarky comments still had a tendency to echo in my head when I was feeling unsure about myself. These days, she had a lot to say about the way I was living my life.

"He asked me on a date," I mumbled, looking away.

Cassie's face brightened and she sat up and bounced in place. If she hadn't been holding a glass, she would have been clapping. "Oh, yay! Did you say yes? Tell me you said yes, that man is scrumptious. And so perfect for you!" Her excitement waned when she finally saw the expression on my face. "You said no? Why?" She sounded surprisingly like Aurie when she whined.

"I'm busy! You know, the store, and I just got a new client who needs me to find this really cool first-edition treatise on witches in the Middle Ages. I don't have time to date anyone, no matter how scrumptious."

"Juliette! Are you serious?"

"Hey," I protested, "you're one to talk! Isn't that exactly the reason you didn't want to date Sam?"

Cassie blushed. "Well, yeah, but I listened to my friends and my family, and I changed my mind." She looked so happy it almost made me change mine.

You are not cute and bubbly like your cousin. You are many layers of prickliness covering a hard, cold center. Okay, that was a little harsh. *Doesn't change the fact that you're hard to love. Every single person who has ever tried can't be wrong, right?*

Something of my inner dialogue must have shown on my face because Cassie put her drink down and leaned in toward me. Placing her hands on my knees she looked me dead in the eyes. "Juliette, I don't know nearly enough about your past, something I am determined to remedy by the way, so I'm making a wild guess here and I might be completely off base. I want you to know that whoever has made you feel like you are not worthy of love was wrong. You are an incredible, funny, smart, and loveable woman. And you deserve to be happy. Stop telling yourself otherwise."

"I'm happy!" The first thing she'd said hurt too much to focus on, but she was wrong about her last point.

"I know! I know you love your shop and working with my dad and me. But you deserve more than that in your life." Her smile was so gentle, it almost made me scream.

"My life is fine." The firmness in my voice made her lean back. "No, my life is wonderful. I love my new shop, and I'm getting more and more clients who need me to locate really interesting artifacts and books. Plus, I have you, Aurie, and our friends. I have everything I could ever want."

"Okay." She held up her hands in surrender. "I believe you. I'm sorry I said anything. I just..." Her eyes sought Sean out in the crowd and mine followed. Glancing back at me she shrugged. "I just want more for you."

The emptiness in my heart ached when Sean glanced over at us and met my gaze. I tore my eyes from his and smiled at Cassie. "I don't need more. I have everything I've ever wanted right here."

If you enjoyed <u>Sweet & Sour Spells</u>, please take a moment to leave a rating or review to help other readers discover Cassie's magical world.

Not quite ready to say goodbye to the Portney crew?

Download two bonus chapters to read Cassie's heart-thumping rescue from Juliette's point of view. Download your free extra chapters at https://bit.ly/SweetAndSourSpellsBonusChapters

A Quick Plea

If you enjoyed this book, please take a moment to rate/review this book on Amazon, Goodreads, or wherever you shop for books.

Receive a free booklet of Cassie's recipes when you sign up for my newsletter at blueoctopuspress.com or by scanning the QR code below.

* *The Paranormal Women's Fiction genre was started by 13 fabulous paranormal fiction authors who wanted to write characters more relatable to middle age women. Read more about PWF at paranormalwomensfiction.com.*

About The Author

Jessica Rosenberg is an emerging author of cozy paranormal and fantasy fiction. She writes books she wishes were already written from her home office on the Central Coast of California where she's closely supervised by Axl, the office cat, and Dottie and Sorella, the family dogs. When she's not at her desk, she can be found on the beach looking for sea glass and other treasures.

Printed in the USA
CPSIA information can be obtained
at www.ICGtesting.com
LVHW051702200823
755758LV00043B/711